25 ₡₂

S0-AIX-208

THE DARK MIRROR

Californian private eye Mike Faraday reckons the case is routine, until a silenced gun cuts down Horvis, the antique dealer, and involves Mike in a trail of murder and violence.

Between the violence and the girls—'I never could resist the appeal of a pretty ankle,' says Faraday—sardonic humour enlivens the plot involving Dance Tucker, the big police chief with a penchant for green apples; MacNamara, the sour-faced surgeon who 'looked like someone was burning lino under his nostrils'; and the sadistic Captain Jacoby.

This fast-moving tale is the first to feature Mike Faraday, the gritty detective who makes his living the hard way in downtown L.A.

THE DARK MIRROR

Basil Copper

·BLACK·
DAGGER
·CRIME·

First published 1966
by
Robert Hale Limited
This edition 1991 by Chivers Press
published by arrangement with
Robert Hale Limited

ISBN 0 86220 796 7

British Library Cataloguing in Publication Data available

FOR MY WIFE
ANNIE
With gratitude for her encouragement

Printed and bound in Great Britain by
Redwood Press Limited, Melksham, Wiltshire

FOREWORD

BASIL COPPER trained as a journalist and for the last fourteen years of his career held the position of News Editor. It was not until his career as a journalist came to an end that he turned to freelance authorship and proved himself to be a prolific writer of diverse range.

His first reputation was achieved in the field of the macabre, where he is now an acknowledged master; the titles of his works—*Necropolis, From Evil's Pillow* and *Here Be Daemons*—speak for themselves. His interest in the macabre also embraces non-fiction and he has published scholarly studies of the historical evidence for both the vampire and the werewolf.

His general interest in fantasy also extends to classic detective fiction, and this resulted in his being chosen to continue the Solar Pons series of the late August Derleth which, in his own words, 'combine the traditional detective form with the atmospheric and macabre'.

Together, these two bodies of work would make up a satisfactory writing career for most authors, but Copper has a third and completely separate strand of his work in his invention of the detective Mike Faraday, who has now appeared in fifty-two crime novels.

Faraday is a private detective in downtown Los Angeles, with a shabby integrity, a head for hard liquor, a constant need for money, and a compliant blonde secretary/girl friend. Collectively the Faraday novels are a work of open homage to the hard-boiled wise-cracking school of Southern Californian writers, exemplified by Dashiell Hammett, Raymond Chandler and the dozens of lesser writers who produced the American detective fiction of the 1940s.

The first Faraday novel, *The Dark Mirror*, was originally published in 1966 and it contains all the ingredients of the classic private eye story. It opens with Mike Faraday being employed by an up-market antique dealer to recover an unidentified *objet d'art*, which was in the possession of a man who has now been murdered. Before Faraday can even leave the house, the antique dealer himself is murdered and from then on the pace never slackens as Copper unravels a Byzantine plot of gunmen, greed, beautiful women and policemen, both honest and corrupt, in all their various double and triple crossings.

For a British author to succeed in this specialised and predominantly American field is exceptional, but Basil Copper does have not only an astonishing knowledge of the nuances and interplay of the 1940s' *cinema noir* and the literature on which it was based, but also the ear to recreate its tone of voice and social attitudes, if not always its wisecracks to Chandler's level.

LAURENCE HENDERSON

Laurence Henderson, who succeeded Basil Copper as Chairman of the Crime Writers' Association, was formerly a City executive. One of his thrillers was made into a film starring Oliver Reed.

THE BLACK DAGGER CRIME SERIES

The Black Dagger Crime series is a result of a joint effort between Chivers Press and a sub-committee of the Crime Writers' Association, consisting of Marian Babson, Peter Chambers and chaired by John Kennedy Melling. It is designed to select outstanding examples of every type of detective story, so that enthusiasts will have the opportunity to read once more classics that have been scarce for years, while at the same time introducing them to a new generation who have not previously had the chance to enjoy them.

CONTENTS

AUTHOR'S NOTE

The L.A. of the story is a composite;
any resemblance to an actual city is
coincidental.

B.C.

1

Mr. Horvis

IT WAS HOT in Jinty's Bar, a damned sight too hot for
comfort. Even the ice in my drink looked too tired to compete
any more by the time it reached me. The bar-tender, a middle-
aged ex-baseball player with cropped hair, wearing a crumpled
white jacket that looked as though he'd slept in it, was visibly
wilting.

"Hot," he said impassively as he put my drink down on a
hexagonal fibre mat. A comic. He moved away, wiping invisible moisture from the bar, the way they all do. The long
room was empty except for me and a fat old guy over in
the corner in a pale green suit flecked with mauve, wearing
a Harvard tie. He kept mopping his brilliantly polished forehead with a limp white handkerchief. He looked like a
stranded fish.

The fan in the ceiling seemed almost to warm the torpid
air and its shrill squeak served only to accentuate the heat.
Sweat ran down inside my shirtband as I finished my drink. I
sighed heavily and thought over my day so far.

Not an auspicious start. Three bills and an insulting letter
sat sourly on the mat inside the large office I shared with the
operative from Gimpel's Agency. They dealt mostly with
insurance, bad debts, minor bouncing jobs. Bert Dexter, whose
desk was opposite mine, was a tall, gangling Texan who
seemed to hate his job. I thought most agency men looked

down on my sort of work, but he had an admiring respect that not only made the shared office bearable, but allowed me to think I was in a worthwhile line of business. When he had clients I walked the block, and he reciprocated. What the hell, it halved the rent and it seemed to work.

That morning Bert hadn't showed up for one reason or other. I'd soon read the bills and even killing flies was beginning to lose its charm. I sat back in my old swivel chair, added to the scratch marks on my broadtop desk and counted the stains on the ceiling. Stella only came in every other day when things were slack and this wasn't her day. It wasn't my day either. It was Monday and the morning had that stale, worn look that Mondays often have in L.A., especially in office blocks that have old and poor air-conditioning, worn carpets and elderly lift boys.

So I wasn't too unhappy when the phone buzzed softly round about 11 a.m. I was just about to brew myself up some coffee on the small range in the annexe back of the main office and I made the desk in three seconds flat. It had been almost a month since I had my last definite assignment and I was running short of cigarette money.

"Hullo." The voice was low and oily but with an undertone of rocks in it. "Faraday Investigations?"

I assented smoothly, seating myself in the chair and getting out my scratch pad. Somewhere I could hear milk frying on the range in back but this was no time to attend to it.

"I wish to be connected to the principal," the voice went on unctiously.

I jiggled the phone and made with the sound effects. "Faraday speaking," I said crisply with what I hoped was a note of authority in my voice, mentally blowing myself a raspberry for my snobbery.

"Mr. Michael Faraday?" the voice went on. This was getting monotonous. We should be on come Thanksgiving at this rate. He was off the bumf at last.

"My name is Adrian Horvis. I wish to engage your services in a somewhat delicate matter."

"How delicate?" I queried, my mind adjusting itself to the prospect of eating full-time.

There was a moment of long hesitation. I could smell the folding money clear across from where he was phoning.

"Shall we say, too delicate to discuss fully on the phone, Mr. Faraday."

His voice had a definite edge to it. I sat back and waited for him to speak again. I scratched my instep with my pencil where it itched beneath my thin sock and watched a spider tracing fancy patterns on the edge of the sun blind. From the street a car back-fired and a motor scooter, like an agitated gnat, went fretting down the boulevard. My caller was speaking again.

"Might I know what your fees would be, Mr. Faraday? Full-time, that is."

I told him. The name was beginning to click with me now and I upped the rate by twenty-five per cent. As we talked I leafed through the L.A. Business Directory. There was a short puff of indrawn breath when I named the fee and another silence. I was beginning to get irritated and the conversation was boring me.

"Your fees come high, Mr. Faraday."

"No one's twisting your arm," I told him. "I work on results. No joy, no fee, other than nominal out-of-pocket expenses."

Horvis brightened, as far as a voice like his could.

"Eminently reasonable, Mr. Faraday. I think we can take it as settled, then."

"Not so fast," I said. "Let's quit horsing around. I haven't said I'll take the job yet. I shall have to know quite a bit more than I know now, and I'm told the city phone rates are going up in the fall. It's going to be pretty cold in this office with all that snow around."

He almost laughed at this. "Tut-tut, Mr. Faraday. Please don't be impatient. I would like you to meet me to discuss the nature of my business. But I can say that it is connected with the Braganza affair. . . ."

The rest of his sentence fell with a thud into the air. I took a moment or two to register, then I had it.

"You mean the guy that got his ass all shot to pieces over on Sunset Canyon?" I asked.

"Picturesquely put, Mr. Faraday," Horvis said dryly. "But substantially correct in outline. My interest in this matter is most intimate, I can assure you. And the pay would be good— on results, of course."

"It would have to be on this caper," I said.

"Would five hundred suit you as a small retainer? And there would be more to follow."

It would and it was. I made up my mind on the spot.

"Why did you contact me in particular?"

A dry chuckle. "I got your name from Charlie Snagge. He said you were a good man."

Things began to add up. I had worked with Charlie Snagge out of the County Sheriff's Office a half dozen years before and he was a good man too.

"All right, Mr. Horvis," I said more cheerfully. "I'll be by around half past three this afternoon, if that will suit you."

"Admirable," he said. "This is in strictest confidence, of course."

I took down his address on my pad, thanked him and hung up. When I had mopped up the mess in the annexe I put some fresh coffee on to brew and considered just what I knew. That didn't take long so I rang Charlie Snagge. He knew Horvis, mainly as a witness in the Braganza shooting. He seemed reliable enough; solid, respectable, wealthy. It appeared he had a business appointment with the dead man, but he never showed up.

When I had thanked Charlie and gone back to my coffee, the room seemed twice as bright, the pile on the carpet fresh and unworn and even the spider seemed to be benevolent as he jiggled in the dusty sunlight. It was now around noon and I had a little checking to do. I read Horvis's address again; 2168 Avocado Boulevard. It appeared to be over to the north

of town, about a twelve-mile drive into the hills. I turned back
to the commercial directory; Horvis, Adrian. Fine art dealer
and antiquarian. It gave a swank address on one of the smartest
boulevards in the business section.

I decided to have a look over there on my way to lunch. I
had an idea Horvis had phoned from home and I wanted
to see what sort of lay-out he had. I put in a call to Stella and
asked her to drop by around six. It looked like being a busy
day, what with one thing and another. I found myself whistling as I went down the hall.

2

My five-year-old powder blue Buick with the tan hide upholstery positively sparkled in the sun, despite the thick white
dust which coated it and the negro attendant on the parking
lot risked a heavy rupture as he rushed to fling open the door
for me. I drove west into the swanky section of town, along
23rd and Maple and presently found a hole in the traffic and
sneaked in to park, risking my bumpers.

I fumigated my upholstery with a Camel and waited. The
place looked pretty good. There was a red and white striped
sun-blind over the top of the window, copper-bronze grille
work and fluting and plenty of cream and white stucco. Inside,
the shop was dim and cool-looking with lots of Chippendale
and that sort of stuff lying about.

I went in and a bell started to play Tchaikovsky's Fifth. A
blonde woman of about forty-five materialized with a soft
swishing sound. She had on steel-rimmed glasses and her bust
would have graced a windjammer.

"Yes?" It was a statement, not a question.

"Mr. Horvis?"

I was taking a chance here but I was pretty sure he wasn't
in.

"I'm sorry." The frost in the voice helped to lower the
temperature. "He doesn't come in on Mondays. Can I
help?"

"Not unless you play pool," I said. "But you haven't the waistline for one thing and your assets might interfere with your shooting angles."

I couldn't help it. Her snooty manner had me riled up. She flushed and her face cracked abruptly.

"Suit yourself." She turned away disdainfully as the bell began to play the opening fanfare from Parsifal. I kept watch as she fussed around an elderly couple with Palm Beach tans. They evidently wanted a Sheraton dining set and the blonde figurehead was trying to shake them down for about three times its real value.

I could see she was winning hands down so I went on out and drove across town. The bell played what sounded like the 1812. Whatever it was, it was derisive. At the Central Library I settled myself into one of their institutional bum-creasers and prepared for a smooth half hour with the *Examiner*. It took me some little while and I didn't find much at that.

It appeared that Cesare Braganza—an unlikely name if ever I heard one—had been shot full of holes and his breath stopped in a lonely spot in Sunset Canyon about two miles off the State Highway. The shooting was close range stuff, from the front, and Braganza, who was forty-nine and described as a dealer in precious stones, had died instantly.

The body might never have been discovered but that a courting couple had chanced that way a couple of nights later. Captain Dan Tucker of the County Police had been assigned, but neither then nor at the hearing which followed had anything ever emerged to identify the killer or killers. Little was known of Braganza or where he came from and no relatives ever came forward.

I sat smoking for a few minutes, puzzling this out. A pert little librarian with a high, tip-tilted bust clip-clopped out, made a moué and pointed energetically to a "No Smoking" sign. I flashed her the old charm smile, putting all I could into it and she went out grinning. I carried on smoking.

I went on through the files. There didn't seem to be much else. Adrian Horvis had been called early in the hearing. He

said Braganza had called at the shop two days before the
shooting and explained he had a pair of jade figurines he
wanted to sell. He was able to prove ownership through documents he carried but these were never found, neither was the
brown leather valise in which he had the figures. Horvis was to
have met him for a further talk but he didn't return. I was
still frowning as I went out and my concentration must have
been terrific because I drew a startled look from the little
librarian.

I made her a courtly bow and went on through the swing
doors. In the booth outside I got Stella at the first ring. No
one had called her at home and she was going to look in at
the office around five. I sat in the car and ruminated on. The
sun threw back a blinding heat from the windshield and even
in the open-top the air was stifling, tasting of gasoline and
foliage, the way it often does in L.A.

After ten minutes a smog started coming on and I drove
over to Jinty's. It was after two when I got outside a sandwich and about twenty to three when I left the bar. I had
allowed myself nearly an hour, mainly in order to tool quietly
along and get the pieces in place. Trouble was there were few
pieces and those wouldn't fit.

I drifted off Highway 44 and turned in over the dirt road
up through the brushwood hills that led to Avocado Boulevard. It wasn't the regular way but I wanted to take in the
countryside. After twenty minutes I hit the metalled road
again. The garish neon of the Jazz Inn, ablaze even in the
hot sunshine of early afternoon swung by and then the Buick
took the corner with a crunch at the intersection of Avocado
and Peartree. I was looking for something pretty high-living
but I had to whistle to myself when I saw it.

There was about three miles of patio-style whitewash wall
and something like a wing of Buckingham Palace sticking up
beyond a fringe of catalpa trees. Next door, in an open-style
lot modelled on an English garden with closely manicured
lawns, an old guy stood in a tennis court set against one of
Horvis's inner walls. He wore pink linen slacks, white sneakers

and a canary yellow open-neck shirt. He evidently thought himself hot stuff.

He was playing tennis with himself against the high wall, despite the heat and not making a bad job of it. I drove on round the block and when I passed again, he missed a shot. He threw the racket on the ground and danced a gopak. The Buick drifted up the drive and stopped in front of a twenty feet flight of marble steps. I was sweating when I got to the top. Below me, the drive curved round a shoulder of hill and I could see a negro chauffeur hosing down one of two cars. I was impressed despite myself. Horvis himself answered my ring.

"Lot of money in the junk business," I said. He didn't flinch. He was a shortish man, stoop-shouldered, wearing a white tropical suit with a pale blue polka-dot tie. He showed a lot of expensive bridgework when he smiled. It was about five millimetres wide.

"Ha! Mr. Faraday." He laughed mirthlessly. "You have a great sense of humour. Come along in."

He waved a hand expansively and I followed him across a hall the size of a small aerodrome. Grey marble, black and white tiles, a cedarwood patio with plants which gave off a sickly perfume; there was even a small fountain playing in the middle. The carpet in the lounge which opened up off the patio was of mustard yellow. It stretched for several acres and the pile almost caught me behind the knees.

"Quite a lay-out," I said reluctantly, instantly regretting my heavy praise.

Mr. Horvis's lips opened deprecatingly and he gave a slight shrug. A snap of the fingers produced a Filipino houseboy in a white coat who glided noiselessly across the carpet as though on castors. He probably was at that.

"A drink, Mr. Faraday?"

I assented to a modest Scotch and allowed myself to be steered to a divan about a block and a half long. The whole place was like Xanadu in Citizen Kane and I kept waiting for the camera boom to come down out of the ceiling. But it didn't so I said nothing and waited for Horvis to speak.

He took his time about it, and it was some while after the drinks had appeared, again borne by the rubber-footed Filipino, before he spoke again.

"What do you know about the Braganza shooting, Mr. Faraday?" The oily voice was free from guile, but I never felt at ease with Mr. Horvis in the short time I knew him. So I swilled my drink around and gazed up at the ceiling before I replied.

"Only what I read in the papers. He was shot about six times wasn't he? Nobody knew anything about him and the marksman was never found."

Mr. Horvis seemed satisfied. He crossed his immaculately clad legs and looked seriously at his mustard yellow floor.

I went on, "You had a business deal with Braganza, paid him off and your cheque was found on him after he was cooled. You were in the clear."

Mr. Horvis fingered his nose thoughtfully and commenced to pick it as though he were alone.

"Yes, quite so, I was in the clear." He sighed heavily and got up abruptly, putting his glass down on a crystal table that would have cost me a year's salary and then some. He walked nervously up and down and intently examined an arrangement of lines and oblong shapes preserved in a plain wood frame over the fireplace.

"I have engaged your services, Mr. Faraday . . . because you have, shall we say, a certain reputation. . . ."

I said nothing and continued downing my drink. Mr. Horvis shot me a sudden glance and continued.

"A reputation, if I may say so, for integrity in business dealings and a certain, er . . . resilience in difficult situations."

I encouraged him. "What do you want, Mr. Horvis?"

He looked pained and his hand fingered his nose again. "All in good time, Mr. Faraday. I had further business with Mr. Braganza. He was to have sold a rather valuable item for me. We met on the second occasion and I handed it over. He was to have brought back the cash."

He fidgeted awkwardly with the edge of the carpet. "As you know, he never turned up. Someone probably has both the article and the money. Either way I want one or the other, but preferably the article."

"Why didn't you tell all this to the police?" I asked.

"Mr. Faraday!" The surprise was genuine. "A man in my position with many contacts in the art world cannot afford to be involved in scandal. No, sir, I had to be discreet."

"What was this business?" I persisted. "And what is this article you seem so anxious to keep under wraps?"

Mr. Horvis pursed his lips in a prim and somewhat unusual manner. He kept his eyes fixed on the ceiling.

"Again—to protect both buyer and seller—I am not in a position to reveal the details."

I got to my feet. "Thanks for the drink, Mr. Horvis," I said and started towards the door.

"Mr. Faraday!" Mr. Horvis was shocked. He almost ran after me across the yellow carpet.

"Don't bother to see me out," I said. "I can find my own way."

"You mean you won't take the case?"

"Let's cut out all the poop," I told him. Pale red spots blazed on either cheek, but he made no answer. "What you need is a gypsy fortune-teller, not an investigator," I said.

Mr. Horvis heaved a long sigh and mastered himself with an effort. "You are quite right, Mr. Faraday, it was a silly gambit on my part. Please forgive me. The whole thing is most delicate, most delicate; and concerns other interests than my own. Please have another drink."

We returned to the table and I stood waiting while he poured the Scotch. Then I leaned against the plinth of a writhing bronze which disfigured that corner of the apartment and gave him a long look as I drank. He shifted uneasily and went back to the fireplace. The arrangement of lines and blobs seemed to have an inordinate interest for him.

"Let's level, shall we?" I asked him. "Suppose I give you a lead. Let's assume this object, as you put it, is of great value. It would have to be, to go to all this trouble. Then let's say it's illegal or you would have called the police. . . ."

Horvis was silent after I finished speaking. Our cigarette smoke went up slowly, hardly wavering in the warm, still air.

"Well done, Mr. Faraday," he said at length. "Seven out of ten, I should say. I cannot afford to be named in this matter."

"I see that," I said. "Even so, you live pretty high for a receiver."

Mr. Horvis choked and the red spots were back in his cheeks. He took two paces forward. "How dare you!" he spluttered.

"Take it easy," I told him. "No offence. Assume that I'm wrong about you, that you're in this right up to your altruistic neck, simply for the love of beauty and art."

"Sarcasm doesn't become you, Mr. Faraday," he said, with a faint sneer.

"Very well, Mr. Horvis. Let's get down to cases. You want me to recover an object—details unknown. Before I start I want to know a few more things."

He smiled slightly. "Then you will take the case?"

"Yes," I said. "Providing that I'm not actually breaking the law. What I find and my subsequent actions depend on how the chips fall."

"Fair enough," he said. He moved to an ornate desk at the side of the fireplace. "Let's get to business, shall we? A down payment on your services. In return I'll give you a rundown on Braganza and you can take it from there."

He sat down and scribbled something in a long pink cheque book. He dried the ink on a blotter and handed me the slip. I put the five hundred in my billfold. It felt about two feet thick and added to my security no end. A door shut softly somewhere in the house and an odd look of strain came back into Horvis's eyes. He drew me to one side.

"Would you mind stepping into the conservatory for a moment, Mr. Faraday?" He shut the door behind me among a welter of fleshy-leaved plants. "I have one or two things to attend to."

I looked idly about me. The conservatory was about forty feet long and like something out of a jungle nightmare. Bulbous plants writhed towards the roof and the air steamed oppressively. A side door led to another glass annexe and then a sort of porch led to the open air. Through the distorted atmosphere of several layers of glass I could see the negro chauffeur far off in the distance. He was polishing the second car. I started to sweat and after a few minutes I got bored.

As I got to the conservatory door and yanked it open I heard a soft pop in the silence, something like a car backfire. I walked over to a picture window and could see the car itself, a black sedan parked down near my Buick at the foot of the steps. It slid out while I was watching and disappeared down the boulevard. I walked back into the lounge.

Mr. Horvis was lying quite near the desk where I had left him. Powder burns had left big yellow scorches round the crimson hole in his chest and little bubbles of blood were still coming from his mouth and spilling across the yellow carpet. His eyes were open and surprised and his little teeth beneath the relaxed upper lip gave him the look of a dead ferret. I didn't need to look any farther and I had no intention of touching him.

Whoever had been at work on him, presumably the gentleman in the black sedan, knew his job. He had been shot with a silencer at very close range. My belly muscles were already fluttering, as they always did in the presence of death.

I walked over to the desk. Incredibly, the Filipino houseboy worked on in the kitchen undisturbed; I could hear him swilling water far off. Not so surprising really, considering that I hadn't heard much either. Nice work, fella, I told myself. No client, no fee, no case. I glanced down at the carpet. So long, Mr. Horvis. I took out the cheque and tore it up and then put the pieces carefully in my pocket. I would burn them later. A glance at the cheque book and I saw that he had not yet entered the payment on the stub. He had written the cheque on the desk surface and there was no impression on the slip underneath.

I tore out the corresponding stub. The numbers wouldn't match, but sometimes people lost cheques or tore them out completely. It would be a minor point. I had my licence to consider. The Filipino houseboy had seen me, of course; I couldn't get round my visit to the house but no one could say that I hadn't left before the unpleasantness. I tore out the blotter too. Better to make sure. I picked up my glass and carried it quietly through into the conservatory; the old boy next door in the pink slacks was still doing his Nijinsky act with the tennis racket. He never looked up.

I found a tap connected up to a plastic hose and swilled out the glass. I dried it on my handkerchief and put it back among the others. I don't know why I bothered because the houseboy would remember bringing us the drinks. I glanced at my watch. It was about fifteen minutes since the shot and I had to hit the trail. I swore under my breath. Some case. I took a final glance around the lounge and then pussy-footed rapidly back to the conservatory. With a bit of luck I could make it to the Buick without being spotted by the chauffeur. The conservatory door opened soundlessly and a few seconds later I was through the outer door and into the open air. I straightened up, one hand on the door handle as a big, beefy foot encased in tan brogues clamped down with crushing force on my toes. An enormous form surmounted by a green pork-pie hat blocked out the sky.

"Hullo, Mike. Going some place?" said Dan Tucker.

2

Dan Tucker

CAPTAIN DAN TUCKER's leathery face, scored and traced as though with a fine knife, wore a broad grin, but a frosty glint in his grey eyes belied the humour. He wore a pale yellow bow tie with red dots and his bulky body was impeccably sheathed in a grey lightweight suit. He made no effort to get off my foot and we stared at one another for perhaps five seconds, while my mind slipped its ratchet.

"Do you think I could have my foot back?" I asked mechanically. "I'd like to use it again some time."

"Sorry, boy," rumbled Tucker gustily. "I thought the floor was a bit uneven."

He was unashamedly enjoying the situation. Though he could be ruthless, he was a fair man if you treated him right. I decided to level with him. This was one of the times, obviously, where you treated him right. I sighed and moved away from the doorpost.

"Come on in," I said. "I was just on my way to call a cop."

"You've come to the right shop," he said. "Phone broke down, I suppose?" There was no trace of sarcasm in his voice. He picked a grape gloomily as we went through the conservatory and spat a pip noiselessly into the bucket as we passed.

"How did you get here?" I asked, fumbling with the door into the house.

"Someone just phoned in," he said. "I took the call in the car about two blocks away. Anonymous."

Helpful. Real helpful. Tucker's voice was entirely without inflexion, giving the conversation a curiously detached feeling. We passed the picture window. A black and white prowl car was parked at the front of the steps. The bonnet was slewed right across the front of my Buick. A very tough-looking cop sat at the wheel of the police car and munched an apple. Another was taking a look at my licence details. I was glad I had the torn-up cheque in my pocket.

"He needn't have bothered," I said, hoping to sound light-hearted. "I was coming to tell you."

We passed into the lounge and stopped. Horvis was still lying where I'd left him. He was hardly likely to have moved. This wasn't the movies but it would have been very convenient if someone had cleared him up. The Filipino for instance. My luck was right out.

"Dear me," said Tucker. He took off his hat.

"Very touching," I said.

He took a small green apple from his pocket and began to crunch it in strong white teeth. It made a vivid crackling noise in the silence and the heat.

"Do you have to?" I asked.

"Very good for the teeth," he said. "The D.A. likes a nice clean force."

His eyes were darting about the room as he spoke. I felt his gaze stabbing at the desk, the cheque book, the area round the body, before he stepped to the window. He rapped on the glass and one of the cops came up the lawn. He came on the double. I was impressed. Tucker found a small lattice pane and opened it. Snatches of conversation came back to me intermittently. I went and sat on the sofa and poured a drink and got my story ready. The cop saluted Tucker and disappeared round the side of the house at a run.

"A relative?" I asked. Tucker ignored the irony. He went heavily to the phone. An apple core spun through the air and landed neatly in Horvis's waste basket.

"Ten out of ten," I said. "Give the gentleman a grape."

Tucker dialled and I sat looking at the lines and blobs on the wall over the fireplace. I still couldn't make them out. I looked at Horvis again.

"He won't keep this weather," I told Tucker.

"I've just taken care of that," he said. Outside, through the now open window I could hear the prowl car spitting tinny instructions into the quiet afternoon, heavy with static and what sounded like bursts of music. There was a sudden jabber of noise in the kitchen and the second cop was talking to the Filipino; a figure in livery went round the side of the house at a run. He came up towards the window but Tucker waved him off. He dialled another number.

"Yes, sir," I heard him say. "Name Faraday. Naw, I think he's okay. Anyway, I'll go work him over. Ring you back. 'Bye."

He put the phone down heavily and stumped back towards me. He sat down in a chair opposite, took out another apple and sank his teeth into it.

"All right, gumshoe," he said. "Start talking. But it had better add up." The smile at the back of his eyes belied his tone.

"Braganza," I said. His eyes widened.

"It figures. I'm glad you said that. Your licence. . . ."

I put down my licence, my driving permit and a pile of other documents on the glass table. He let them lie.

"You carry a gun?" He took another bite on his apple and I looked up at the ceiling.

"No," I said. "Least, not normally. I did a little judo during the war."

Tucker took another bite and said nothing.

"Do you want to search me?" I asked.

Tucker sighed and crossed his legs. He gave me a long look.

"Not necessary. Strangely enough, I believe you. But I am curious about some things. This may take some time."

"I'm not going any place," I said.

There was the noise of a car engine out in the drive, doors

slamming and voices. A sergeant of detectives came in with the Filipino. He was protesting but shut up when he spotted Horvis on the floor. His eyes looked sick. Two men in the white coats of the city ambulance service came in with a stretcher and went in a side room to wait. There were more comings and goings. A police surgeon, a thin, sour-faced man named MacNamara came in with a small bag, spoke affably to Tucker and gave me a chill nod.

He fussed around the body. Print men began dusting furniture; the body was examined again and Tucker excused himself. He went to join the small knot of men round the heap on the floor. Flash bulbs winked and notebooks were flourished. This carnival went on for about an hour and then the crowd began thinning out. MacNamara went on out to wash up.

"Report by 6 p.m.," he snapped to Tucker. He never looked at me. He went on out, treading warily on the carpet. He looked like someone was burning old lino under his nostrils. The phone went again. Tucker answered it.

"No," he said. "Have the calls diverted. No statement at present. I'll prepare something for the Press later this afternoon. 'Bye."

He rejoined me near the table. Another apple core flicked through the air. This time it missed the basket and fell on the carpet. The two white-coated attendants came in. Horvis was placed on the stretcher and covered with a sheet. They took him on out. Presently the door slammed and then the siren went wailing up Avocado Boulevard. The morgue lay that way.

I started talking. I told Tucker about my call from Horvis, my line of investigation so far, the earlier part of our conversation.

Tucker was regarding me suspiciously. "And you're sure he had no time to tell you anything? You were here nearly an hour, the Filipino tells me."

"Something happened," I said. "I think he heard someone come in. Anyway, he turned me out in the greenhouse for about twenty minutes."

"And you sat there eating grapes in that heat, I suppose, all the time?"

"I stood outside the porch for a bit," I said.

"And you became suspicious when he stopped breathing, I take it?"

"My ears aren't that good," I said. "I heard a sort of pop and saw the car drive off. That's when I came back. You know the rest."

Tucker sighed heavily again. "All right," he said. "This'll do for now. But don't leave town."

"Sure," I said. "I was flying out to Palm Beach when you turned up."

The phone rang again. Tucker was rather longer this time. When he put down the receiver he sat blowing his cheeks in and out and frowning so hard you could see the creases chasing way across his face like storm clouds on a hill.

"Trouble?" I said.

"I'm used to it. That was Sergeant Gibbs. They traced the black sedan you saw leaving. Hired from a garage about two miles from here. Guy paid on the spot, left no address."

"Description?"

Tucker shrugged. "Sure. Medium. Medium sort of guy, medium height, medium build. Wore a grey suit."

"Helpful," I said.

He started biting another apple. I figured he must have a bushel basket stashed somewhere in back of his pants.

"So what are we sitting here for?" I said. "Let's get out and find him."

Tucker silently ejected a pip from the corner of his capacious mouth, caught it on the back of his hand and spun it into an ashtray.

"You'll get diarrhoea if you keep on with those," I told him.

"Best medicine there is," he said. "Keep the old bowels ticking over. I'll live to be a hundred with these."

I figured he might at that. Just when I was thinking that maybe he'd gone to sleep, he'd been quiet with his eyes shut so long, he suddenly got up, took me by the arm and drew me over to the side of the big lounge.

"Take a look at this, Mike." There was another porch which connected with the garden and corresponded to the one on the other side of the house, leading to the conservatory.

"He came in through here."

I grunted. "Looks as though Horvis may have been expecting company. It wasn't locked?"

"So far as we can make out. No prints, though. Nothing useable."

He pointed down the garden. The chauffeur, one or two policemen and a loafer stood in a small knot discussing the day's proceedings. Tucker rapped on the window and the group broke up. The policemen hustled about, making with the efficiency. Tucker indicated another drive, partly screened by trees, which led from the porch and away in the direction of the steps and my car.

"Dead straight run for the getaway," said Tucker. I led the way back to the couch and poured another drink. Tucker waved the proffered glass away. "I'll stick to apple-juice."

I stared at my toecaps; one side of my left shoe was heavily scuffed, the leather scratched.

"What say we pool our ideas?" I asked Tucker.

"Thought you were off the case now. No client."

He glanced towards the fading stains on the carpet. I figured they'd take a couple of thousand off its value. I ignored his remark.

"What about this sedan?" I persisted.

Tucker scratched his chin. "Looks as though the driver wore gloves. Nothing but dead ends. . . ."

"This woman at the antique shop," I asked. "Built like Charley's Aunt."

"She's all right," said Tucker. "We went into all that last time. So far as I can make out she has a part-interest in the business."

"So what do we come up with?" I went on. "Fact one; Braganza shot by person or persons unknown. Weapon, a silent revolver. Horvis implicated in some way. Fact two; Horvis shot. Weapon, a silenced revolver. Again, no name on the bullet. The shootings must be connected."

"Just my conclusions," said Tucker with grim dissatisfaction. He shot me a sudden glance. "If you do come up with anything, Mike, or anyone contacts you, I want to hear about it. Understand?"

"Perfectly," I told him. "And incidentally, Dan, thanks for believing me."

He smiled thinly. "Just for the record, there never was any doubt in my mind. The call came too pat for that—a public phone booth, of course. But you're such a self-satisfied bastard, I thought I'd leave you on the hook for a bit."

"That figures too," I said, grinning back.

He smiled again and indicated my documents on the table. "Don't forget those. And if you're going to stay on the job I'd take to carrying a gun, if I were you."

I stashed my cards in my breast pocket. "I'll check with you around midday tomorrow," I said.

He nodded again. "I'm staying here to kick things around a bit," he said. "Remember what I said about not leaving town."

I walked across towards the door as Tucker started on another apple. The Filipino came in with a tray loaded with silver dish covers. I caught the aroma of French fried. Tucker munched steadily as the Filipino put the tray down. He went out, looking curiously about him.

"Pity about your client," Tucker said, tentatively lifting up one of the dish covers. "He had his good points."

"So did Hitler," I told him and went on out.

When I got in the fresh air I looked at my watch. It was close on six, but I felt like I had been in there around five years. On impulse I tiptoed back to the picture window and peeked through. There were two apple cores on the floor beside the waste basket and Dan Tucker was just lifting his second dish cover.

2

The Buick was red hot to the touch from being in the sun all that while, but the day was beginning to lose its heat. The car had obviously been given a thorough going over by the police and the contents of the dash pockets had been disarranged, but the cops were civil enough and reversed out of the way as soon as I appeared. I gave them good day and drove off. I needed some time for thinking and took a longer way back to town.

A slot appeared in the parked autos in front of Jinty's and I tooled in. A couple of hundred feet of Caddy turned off at an angle. The driver wound down his window and gave me a Bronx cheer. His face matched the puce of the car's bodywork. His shouted words were lost in the crackle of exhausts. I went on in and sat down at the bar.

There were perhaps a couple of dozen people in and a piano was playing somewhere, the low tinkle coming and going between cracks in the conversation. Everyone looked hot and the fan was still creaking. The bar-tender put down my drink and mopped away at his invisible beer spillings. His white coat looked more crumpled than ever.

"Hot," he muttered as he moved away.

"You want a re-write man on your dialogue," I told him. His face remained blank. Blabbermouth. I sat for maybe three, four minutes thinking out the day and then went into a booth. Stella answered the first ring. I told her I'd be right in.

The office was cooler than the bar. Stella made some coffee and sat swinging her long legs on the desk, looking curiously down into her cup. She said nothing and I was content to leave it like that. The traffic slid past on the boulevard with the cool sussuration that it has on very hot days when the main rush is over and everyone's quietly tooling home, the panic finished. The other half of the office was empty, the typewriters sheathed in their hoods, desk neatly tidied. The insurance boys liked an early day.

Stella winked. "How was it?" she asked.

"We just lost a client," I told her. She just sat there swinging her legs. Stella was a honey blonde with all the right statistics. Some day I figured I'd make her when she was in the right mood, but she was a girl with her mind set on marriage. Either way it was an interesting contest. I admired her legs for perhaps a couple of minutes more and then lit a cigarette. What the hell, it was too hot anyway. Between puffs, I told Stella the story; what there was to know of it.

As I went along I came to realize just how little I had to go on. Two murders which had to be connected—but how? I almost felt sorry for Dan Tucker. I could please myself but he had to come up with something. Thinking of Horvis reminded me of something else and I took out the pieces of the cheque; Stella'e eyes widened as I showed her the figure. She stopped swinging her legs.

"Useful," she said.

I put the pieces in the ashtray and set fire to them. We both watched them smoulder.

"Don't worry," I told her. "I can meet your salary for the next two weeks."

She laughed. "Have some more coffee."

I felt better at the second cup and went over to the window and looked down into the street; the cooler air was coming in from the hills now and the blind was beginning to rattle. The air felt good.

"I almost forgot. Your calls," said Stella. She shoved a slip of paper at me. "I don't think the first's important, but the second might be interesting."

I glanced at the paper. The first was from Charlie Snagge and gave his number. I made a note on my scratch pad for the morning. The second call did seem more interesting. It was from a Miss Sherry Johnson and gave a Park Plaza number. I lit another cigarette. "Know what she wants?"

"She wouldn't tell me. She said for you to call as soon as you came in."

I simulated interest. "Probably popped a stay button and wants me to trace it. What'd she sound like?"

"Stella grinned. "Just your type. I'd say. Sounded nice. Youngish I should think."

I made a succulent noise and finished my coffee. I went around the desk to sit down when Stella said, "There was something in tonight's edition."

She handed me the L.A. *Examiner*. She had ringed a small stick of type on page three of the late edition. Apparently the night editor hadn't considered it very important. It just said that Horvis, well known L.A. antique dealer had been found shot at his home. From the tone of the paragraph it might well have been an accident or suicide. Right at the bottom of the piece there was a two-line stick; Michael Faraday, local City P.I. is helping the police with their inquiries.

I sank back into my chair and dialled the Park Plaza number; I had come well out of that, anyhow. But it was annoying to be linked with Horvis. Whoever was interested would know that I was involved. Though I wouldn't be much longer if I didn't get a break. There was a long burring. Stella went and stood by the window. She had on a white cotton frock with blue polka dots, that set off her figure to perfection. She had lovely legs and everything to go with them. I'll bet she hasn't much on underneath that, I thought, when I caught sight of her smiling reflection in the window glass. A girl's voice was at the other end of the line; it was low, pleasant, well modulated. I put her age at around twenty-four.

"Faraday," I told her. "I understand you rang me earlier."

I heard her catch her breath in relief. "Oh, thank you for ringing, Mr. Faraday. I need help badly. I wonder if you could come over?"

Stella picked up the intercom. phone and sat down at her pad.

"What exactly is your business?"

"I'm afraid I can't discuss that over the phone, Mr. Faraday. It is urgent. I happened to see your name in the newspaper this afternoon and looked you up in the directory."

"All right, Miss Johnson," I told her. "Will around nine o'clock tonight suit you?"

Stella took down the address as she dictated it; it was a swanky hotel block over on one of the main sections. I thanked her again and rang off. Stella tapped her pencil against very white teeth. "Well, Mike?" she asked.

"I don't know," I said slowly. "I've got a strange hunch that this may be connected with Horvis. If it is it will be the first break I've had up to now. I must get back and change, grab a quick bite and take a look at Queen Brunnhilde over at the antique shop. Get me her address will you?"

I slopped some water over my face while Stella did this. "She lives over the shop," she said eventually. "Mrs. Margaret Standish."

"We're full of surprises tonight," I said. "Of course. It would be safer if Horvis had got anything to hide. He could stash it with her."

"You be careful," said Stella.

"Naturally," I said, on my way to the door.

"Seriously, Mike," said Stella, bringing her face close to mine, "take care." Her lips were warm on the side of my face. I put my hand approvingly over the softness of her rump, felt her stiffen and slide away and then she aimed a playful blow at my ear.

"Right," I said and went on out.

Back in the Buick the air was cooler. I drove with the radio going softly. Neon signs were beginning to split the dusk and I had to go carefully at intersections where the lights were beginning to merge with the red of traffic signals. I lived over on Park West in a small, rented house that stood in a row of bijou-type cottages, each cut off by identical open lawns and short laurel hedges.

As I came up the hill, taking in the night air and a dash of Duke Ellington, another car drifted down. There was a blaze of headlights, etching trees, street, houses briefly, like a film negative. I got out of the car without bringing it up to the car-port and walked up the cement path to the house. My near neighbour's house farther up the hill was in darkness, but next door there were lights and what sounded like a football commentary. The family were crouched in the living-room watching television, judging by the blue tribal light. I went on in and cooked myself a small grill while I shaved and changed my shirt. Then I carried the meal into the living-room on a tray and switched my small radio on.

There was a lot of stuff about U.N.O. and what de Gaulle was doing over in Europe and then the local news; there was a short rundown on the Horvis shooting. Still no mention of murder and, best of all, no tie-up with the Braganza kill. I switched off and carried my plates back into the kitchen, rinsed them through and put them in the rack to dry.

It was a pleasant house and suited my needs perfectly. It was well surrounded by neighbours, including two senior cops and I had the front drive and back lot wired for floodlighting in case of prowlers. Short of an Alsatian and electrified fences I couldn't think of anything better. It was now slightly short of eight and I just had time to see Mrs. Standish before getting over to see the girl.

The last thing I did before I left was to go to a locked cupboard in my bedroom. I had a small armoury, consisting of three revolvers and a telescopic-sighted rifle, in there. I chose my old favourite, a Smith and Wesson ·38. As an afterthought I screwed on the silencer and put the whole thing in a nylon holster which fitted beneath the fold of the arm. I felt pretty silly, but like Stella said, you have to be careful. Dan Tucker had given me the same advice too, come to that. It was when I was out on the porch, going to lock up, that I felt the roughness of the door.

I went back inside and switched on the outer light. It burned white in the darkness, outlining me on the porch. It was my night off, so far as sense was concerned. The surface of the door was all scored and splintered, and the lock plate scratched and gouged. Someone had been at work with a pretty hefty jemmy. When I had got this far I suddenly remembered the car which came down past me and the way my headlamp beam had thrown its light way up the hill; it must have been visible for nearly half a mile.

B

It took me just two seconds to get the door between me and the street and to douse the porch light. I gummed my eye to the crack and hit the floodlight switch. All the front drive and the entire surrounding area sprang starkly into blinding detail, every blade of grass distinct underneath the string of heavy duty lamps. I stood motionless in the darkness behind the door, alert for any movement. A tap dripped in the kitchen, somewhere on the back lot a cicada started up its mournful chirp. Nothing moved in all the wide world. Just as suddenly all the tension evaporated. I knew there was nothing there. And behind the door, in the darkness as I doused the floodlights, I began to laugh. Fumbling Faraday had begun to deal the cards right.

Somewhere out there in the night of L.A., down among the smog and neons I was beginning to worry someone. And it could only be the Mr. Big who was tied in with the whole shooting match. For the first time since that morning I was placing my feet without breaking omelettes. I felt convinced the silenced weapon I was looking for was still in L.A. after all. I walked down the drive with confidence and survived with hardly a tremor when my neighbour suddenly let go with a half a truckload of trash cans on his back lot. The Buick sprang to life first pull. The engine roared, full of power and confidence as I turned the car and headed down town, the headlamps slicing the night sky under the palms.

3

Mrs. Standish

THE SKY WAS still blue above the glare of neon when I
pulled up in front of the shop. There was little traffic in the
business section and what there was went by on tip-toe, white-
wall tyres slurring through soft tarmac. I lit a cigarette and
feathered the smoke as I sat in the car; Mrs. Standish seemed
to be home. Lights burned behind pink shades on the upper
floor above the antique shop. I got out of the car and walked
across to the big display windows.

The heat on the sidewalk came to meet me. There were some
shaded lamps burning in the shop, winking back on crystal and
plate and the patina of old things. I searched for a bell pull on
the front door but couldn't find one, so decided to try in back.

The shop was near the end of the block and I walked softly,
keeping into the wall. I had made so many mistakes today I
didn't want to miss out any more. At the end of the block there
was a sort of *patio* set back from the sidewalk, with a strip of
lawn, some trees and fancy shrubs and a couple of car ports.
Along the side of the building there was a wrought iron balustrade with a gate let into it.

I went through the gate and up a flight of stone steps. I felt
exposed as I came out on a small landing, paved with black
and white tiles. A red and white sunblind over a Regency
yellow door with brass fittings re-echoed the style of the front
of the building. I took a glance round the deserted street;

nothing moved for two blocks, not even a solitary car. I thumbed the bell and waited.

Nothing happened, so I tried again. This time there was a response. A yellow light went on quite suddenly, sandwiched between pebble screens. Then, with blinding abruptness, a large brass lantern on the *patio* came to life, making my position about as private as the Yankee Stadium. I looked round the area again and found I was sweating. It wasn't the weather either. After about five years the door opened and a figure appeared in the hallway. It was Mrs. Standish. She wore a red silk dressing-gown and her eyes were dark and swollen. She looked at me uncomprehendingly, blinking in the porch light.

"You wouldn't know me," I told her. "My name's Faraday. Can I come in?"

She hesitated. "It's all right," I said. "Mr. Horvis was my client. I think maybe you can help."

"Nothing can help now," she said in a slurred voice. But she stood aside to let me in. I caught spirits on her breath as I brushed by in the hallway. Inside, the hall was all pastel blue with quilted walls and French prints.

"Haven't I seen you somewhere?" asked Mrs. Standish, looking at me with a blurred eye.

"In the shop," I said. "We didn't hit it off too well."

"Now I remember," she said, looking at me unblinkingly. Then with sudden anger, "You did a good protection job. . . ."

"I wasn't hired for that, Mrs. Standish," I said. "If it helps any, I'm sorry."

She took my arm suddenly and her eyes filled with tears or whisky fumes, or something.

"Don't take any notice," she said. "I didn't mean anything by that. I'm all upset."

Close up and without her glasses she wasn't a bad-looking woman; grief had softened the harsher lines of her face and she looked younger without make-up.

"Come in," she repeated, ushering me forward. "I'm all in a mess." She patted her hair and led the way into a living-room.

This repeated the pattern of the shop but on an even more sumptuous scale. There was crystal and jade and Ming; mahogany tables that reflected back the light, made by English cabinet makers dead this three hundred years; a blue carpet with a pile that made Horvis's look like lino; book cases, cabinets full of china and glass; brass warming pans and all that sort of stuff.

Large divans covered with green silk and piled with cushions made me feel uneasy; all these ottomans and hangings gave the place an Oriental air and I looked around for a brass gong. There wasn't one, but somehow I still felt uneasy. There were dim lights burning in wall brackets of twisted metal and lots more wrought iron balustrades painted pale blue. Through a half-open door lights burned in a bedroom; there was a large bed, half seen, with what appeared to be a white mink coverlet. To complete the M.G.M. touch there was a blue fox fur coat laid casually across the bed.

In one corner the wrought iron descended in a spiral staircase and as I made an appreciative noise at Whistler's uncle who leered at me in a friendly manner from a gilt frame on the opposite wall, I saw that the stairs ended in a hall furnished in the same extravagant manner. Despite the foreshortening I could make out some pretty substantial oak doors covered with an ironwork grille; I guessed, rightly it turned out, that they led to the shop beyond. When locked, they'd turn the place into an isolated apartment, approachable only from the stairway in the street. The rooms had that quiet which is unmistakable. I was certain there was no one else in the flat. I turned back to Mrs. Standish. She was bending over a table and I saw bottles, a cut glass decanter, an array of glasses.

"What's your poison?" she asked.

"Scotch," I said. "With plenty of ice."

I saw something else too. Mrs. Standish bent farther over the table to pour the drinks. She had a pretty good figure. She was naked underneath the gown and I could see way down between her breasts. Any other time I might have been interested but hell, this was no way to respect a woman's grief. Anyway, she didn't give any sign and I transferred my gaze back to Whistler's uncle.

"Hogarth?" I asked.

"Watteau," she said. "Wrong artist, wrong country." Some of the frost had gotten back into her voice. She may have had a few but she was a businesswoman at heart.

"Sorry," I said. "I never majored in art."

"You didn't come here to discuss art?" she queried, interrupting me in a gentle, almost absent-minded manner.

"Well, no," I said, swilling my drink in its frosted glass. "Do you mind if I sit down?"

We sat back on the green silk divan. It was better like that. When she sat down the gown pulled back tight over her breasts. Now I got rid of that temptation I could only see most of her legs. They were bare too and stuck a mile out of the parting of the dressing-gown. I made sure the cord was fastened tightly and transferred my gaze to her shoulder level. They weren't bad legs either, but I had other fish to fry. Besides, I had to save myself for the Johnson girl.

I glanced at my watch and was surprised to find it only a quarter after eight. It sure seemed late. Mrs. Standish took no notice. She took another swig at her drink, which was a long thing with a lot of salad and that sort of junk floating on top of it, and leaned farther back on the divan. She closed her eyes and her voice came from far away.

"What makes you think I can help you, Mr. Faraday? And what's more, what makes you think I'd want to?"

Her voice was unexpectedly sharp, considering the atmosphere and all, that I was at a loss for a moment.

"I've already told the police all I know. I couldn't help them; what do you expect me to say to you?"

I drank some more and shifted my position on the divan. "Supposing you tell me? I might pick up something the cops have overlooked."

She laughed suddenly, a harsh sound which seemed to set the glasses tinkling in the dim room.

"What's the matter, Mr. Faraday? Didn't you collect your fee? Adrian would be amused at that. A real joke. . . ."

She subsided again and started to get outside her drink.

"He did pay me, as a matter of fact," I said evenly. "I tore the cheque up."

Her face dropped and she bit her lip. "I'm sorry I said that," she said, putting her hand on my arm. "I had no right. . . ."

"Forget it," I said. "What is important is for us to talk."

She took another swipe at her drink and wriggled her feet in her slippers. "Why don't you call me Margaret?" she said. "What's your name?"

I told her. "Now that we're Margaret and Michael," I said, "how about some co-operation?"

"What makes you think I know anything?" she persisted.

"I have nothing to go on at all," I said. "Don't you want Horvis's murderer caught?"

Her lips twisted. "What good would it do? If I did tell you anything it would only cause more trouble. There's been enough killing already."

I leaned forward. "Then the two shootings are connected?"

She ignored my remark. "I've said too much. Another drink?"

She poured me another liberal Scotch and mixed herself a second salad mash or whatever it was. She looked at me calmly, swizzling her drink in the glass. Her eyes were quite steady and bright. In the silence the ticking of an ormulu clock sounded like someone breaking rocks.

"Would you like some money?" she asked. "A sort of retainer. Because——"

"No thanks," I interrupted her. "I have a thing about taking money from women. Besides, I'm in this business for the love of it."

"Oh, I'm not offering you a fee to go digging up information no one wants uncovered," she said. "I wouldn't want you to do anything for it."

"In other words you want to buy me off?" I said.

"Something like that."

I put down my drink. "Why is it everyone on this case

wants to let things lie," I said. "Two people get holes drilled
in them and everyone from here clear to Sunset Boulevard
wants to forget all about it. Either disinterest has reached a
high level in this state or it isn't healthy to be too curious. But
I'm starting to worry someone."

I told her about the interrupted attempt to force my door.
She went white and her hand trembled as she hurriedly put
down the drink.

"You think the whole thing's connected?" I asked.

"Don't you?"

"I'm asking the questions," I said.

She drank again. "I suppose it's no use asking you to stop
poking your nose in, fee or no fee?"

"Not a chance," I said. "I'm too curious. Besides, the police
would only go on digging if I didn't."

"I shouldn't rely too much on the police if I were you," she
said dryly. "The L.A. force is full of bad eggs."

"Meaning what?" I said.

"Meaning that sometimes information gets dropped into
pigeon holes," she said.

That set me thinking. We sat quiet and I studied Whistler's
uncle; the leer looked even more pronounced. I had a feeling
that something might break for me tonight but sitting around
wouldn't help. I finished my drink and stood up.

"Thanks for the visit," I said. "And for being so nice."

She looked surprised. And alarmed too, I thought. "You're
not going, surely?"

"I've got to earn a living and the overheads are mounting
up," I said.

"Sit down, Mike, and listen."

I sat down. She made one last try. "You really are going on
with this?"

I said nothing and just stared at her calves; they had a nice
shape. She sighed suddenly.

"All right," she said. "I might be able to help. But nothing
must be traced back to me. About two years ago Adrian started
taking trips and becoming rather mysterious about some aspects

of the business. I used to ask him about them but he would never say much. Then, some months ago, he did take me partly into his confidence. There was an invention, it seemed, in the motor industry, which could be made to yield a lot of money. I don't know the details."

I looked puzzled and she laughed. "Sorry. There was no reason for you to know. Adrian was quite a businessman. The motor connection arises through his brother in Detroit. Leslie is a manufacturer of motor car bodies in a big way."

"Do you think this invention was stolen by whoever murdered Braganza?" I asked.

"Difficult to say. I know so little. But I think it may be likely."

"But despite this you can and will help me?"

"Yes, I can help," she said quietly. "I don't know what the hell this is all about or really why I'm doing it, but I will."

As she went to get up the phone rang from the hall below.

"I won't be a moment," she said and went down the stairs. "Oh, hullo Arthur," she said. "I thought it might be you."

This was an opportunity too good to miss. I went round the room in rapid strides. I concentrated on a small alcove in a corner which seemed to be used as an office. There was a large mahogany bureau there which looked interesting. There was a gilt-framed mirror hanging in the corner and by jumping forward about five feet from the bureau, I could just see Mrs. Standish at the phone; this would be a help in case she came up the stairs suddenly. I don't know what I expected to find, but sometimes you hit the jackpot without meaning to.

The bureau was stuffed full of old receipts, bills, the usual things; a lot of it was an obvious overspill from Horvis's office in the shop. That was another place I should like to give a going over. It would prove difficult though, as it would obviously be wired for an alarm. I riffed through piles of stuff, quite aimlessly, not really knowing what I was looking for. I could hear Mrs Standish rambling on; she was still at the phone but had sat down on the steps of the staircase, with her back to me.

I returned to the bureau. It had long, low drawers in the

front of it, which went way back; they all had keys in the locks. Four of them were unlocked, but the fifth, the second from the bottom, had the key turned. I have a hunch about things like that and in a second I had the drawer open. It slid noiselessly on beautifully fashioned runners.

The drawer contained some magazines, a few odds and ends and, as I pulled it out farther, a couple of big, old, black-bound volumes. I flipped them over languidly and found they were photo albums. Holidays in Maine, days on the beach, the usual. Working swiftly through the years I found an interesting pattern; Mrs. Standish young, Mrs. Standish in her teens; Mrs. Standish in her twenties and thirties with a tall, sad-faced man with a black moustache, whom I took to be Mr. Standish. The second album was more interesting; the photographs were much more recent. Mrs. Standish still looked attractive—strange that I should have thought her matronly and frosty in the shop—but Mr. Horvis had replaced her husband as a companion.

There was one beach shot of her and Horvis; they were good likenesses, obviously taken with an expensive camera and not just a beach photographer's rush job. I slipped the picture out of its mounts and put it in my wallet; she was in a bikini and looked really something and Horvis was in Bermuda shorts; they had their arms around one another.

I was just about to push the drawer back when I saw a big buff envelope. It was right at the back, under the albums, the last thing in the drawer, which is why I almost overlooked it. I have a hunch about things like that, too. Which is why I decided to open it. I didn't learn much about the Horvis shooting but a lot about human nature.

The envelope was full of glossy photographs, obviously self-taken with the same expensive camera. The first pile came roughly in three classes; Mrs. Standish clothed; Mrs. Standish partly-clothed; Mrs. Standish nude. Then they began to get more elaborate. Presently Mrs. Standish was partnered by Mr. Horvis. They were both nude and seemed to be enjoying themselves. The backgrounds were varied; deserted beaches, automobiles, an expensively furnished bedroom or a familiar back-ground crammed with antique furniture. I looked wistfully at Whistler's uncle and eyed the green divan with more respect. This was one of the most entertaining evenings I'd had for some while. I longed to pull up a stool and sit down, but I didn't have the time.

It was when I was holding one of the pictures upside down and squinting at it, that I saw Mrs. Standish. She was at the top of the staircase, one hand on the banister, looking at me intently. She didn't turn a hair. In fact she seemed highly amused. Some woman.

"It goes that way up," she said dryly.

"Thanks," I said. "I see you go in for health cures."

"Perhaps you'd like one of those to go with the other?" she said.

"Good of you," I said. "Next time I could operate the box Brownie. But it wouldn't do for me to be caught with these on the street. Perhaps you could mail them on for me—under plain, sealed wrapper?"

She hooted with laughter and went to pour another drink. "What did you expect to find, Mr. Faraday?"

"I don't know," I said. "Certainly, this was a surprise."

She looked at me in genuine puzzlement. "Why? Because I'm a woman of sensuous appetites and pleasures? I'm no different from anyone else in this world."

"Agreed," I said. "But why perpetuate it in print? These might get in the wrong hands."

She shrugged. "Why not? They're all I have left now."

"A very beautiful friendship," I said.

She flared up momentarily at this. "He was good to me. My husband left me many years ago. Can you blame me?"

I said nothing. She looked at me in silence again. Mrs. Standish shifted where she stood and one of her long, very mature legs came through the parting in her dressing-gown. It looked pretty good.

"You wouldn't like to take me on?" she asked.

"Not tonight," I said. "It's my night for junior scouts."

She gave another throaty laugh. They seemed to be her speciality.

I looked at my watch again. Time was creeping on and I'd talked my ass off for one evening.

"If you dont' mind," I said. "You were going to fetch me something when the phone rang."

"Oh, yes," she said. "I almost forgot."

As though a curtain had been pulled down she suddenly became business-like. She put down the glass and went into the bedroom. Then she called me in. I should have known better. There was a lot of peach and white in the décor and a hell of a lot of that heady French perfume. She was standing in front of a dressing-table and she went to hand me a small white envelope sealed with sticky tape; somehow it slipped out of her hand and went on to the carpet. I got down to pick it up and when I straightened Mrs. Standish had opened up her dressing-gown and as I gawped she let the whole thing slip to the ground.

She was stark naked and calmly stood back for me to admire her. She was silhouetted from every angle in the mirrors around the room; it wasn't like there was anything so very terrific in her figure, but she had that sexy something which is worth all the rest.

"You like?" she said softly. I liked, that was for sure, but this wasn't the night for it. She suddenly stepped forward and all the front of her body came along mine; she cupped my hand on her nipple and her head went back as we kissed. It wasn't so much a kiss as a savage interlocking of our mouths and I felt the dart of her tongue as she bit at me. Then she pushed me quickly away and stood back for me to admire her again.

"I'll save it for you," she breathed.

"You do that," I said, half angry with myself. With a quick movement she bent, scooped up the dressing-gown and covered herself. Then, the gown knotted at the waist, she became again the gracious hostess.

"When?" she asked.

"Soon," I said. "I'll give you a ring."

I turned and went on out. I hadn't got more than two yards when I heard that gurgling laugh again. "You forgot this."

I saw the envelope lying on the carpet where I'd dropped it. St. Peter himself would have dropped his halo this evening. I picked it up and pocketed it.

"Thanks for the drink," I said. "I can see myself out."

I knew I had to get out of the bedroom or I wouldn't have made it. In the hall I paused to straighten my tie in the mirror. It was then that I heard a soft plopping noise. It was the second time that day and it had an electric effect. I went through into the lounge like a tornado. I needn't have worried. Margaret Standish was standing by the bureau with the open envelope of photographs. She had a newly opened bottle in her hand and was pouring herself another libation. She hadn't heard me coming on the soft carpet.

I was sweating again but had to give myself a grin in the mirror as I backed out. I went on the porch and gulped in some night air. I went on down to the street. A clock was striking nine somewhere as I climbed into the seat of the Buick and it felt like another day since I went in. I glanced up but nothing moved behind the pink blinds. The city was still and nothing stirred in the length of the street either.

I got out the envelope and looked at it under the dim light of my dashboard. There was no writing on it, so I tore it open. Inside was something wrapped in several layers of tissue paper. It felt like a flat piece of metal. I unwrapped it and sat staring in the miniscule light cast by the instrument panel. A key was lying in my hand. Just that and nothing more, but I felt a good deal nearer knowing who'd killed Horvis.

It was the key of a safe deposit box. It had a number and the key belonged to the local branch of the Chase National down here in L.A. I put the key in my pocket and lit a cigarette. Then I tore up the envelope and pieces of tissue, walked about ten yards and stuffed them down the nearest storm drain.

Then I drove off. I had an appointment and I was late already.

4

Sherry Johnson

SHERRY JOHNSON lived over in the Bissell Building on Corona Avenue. In L.A. we called it Coronary Avenue on account of the rich old guys living there who sometimes dropped down dead from heart attacks. It was a pretty flash part of town and the commissionaire with the retired rear-admiral's uniform and the fresh laundered white gloves stuffed through the braid of his epaulette gave me a supercilious sniff as my old Buick drifted in through the Parkway.

He didn't bother to come and open the door for me or even to direct me to the parking lot, so I drove on into the apron. He probably thought I was cracker-white. I parked next to a yellow Cadillac that looked like it had gold-plated door handles. It had Texas number plates, so I guess it had at that. I left the car in front of a long board fence; I went on into the lobby of the building. Admiral Dewey didn't even give me another glance. A negro lift boy took me up about two hundred floors.

Two-one-nine was down along a mile of grey-carpeted corridor flanked by lilac-coloured doors. I felt lost without a map and I was pretty well bushed by the time I got to the number I wanted. I blipped the buzzer and waited. The door opened and I stared. I don't know what I'd expected but she was nice. She wore a suit of cornflower blue which seemed to go with her brown hair flecked with gold tints. Her eyes were grey and steady. She had dimples too, as she smiled, which she did right away, revealing regular white teeth.

"My, but you're tall," she said.

"That's my press agent," I said. "All done with built-up shoes."

She opened the door wide and I went on in. It was a nice room. The sky was quite dark now and through the long windows punched in one wall I could see stars like the reflection of the city lights below.

"Sorry I'm late," I said. "I'm Faraday."

"I hoped you would be," she said. I let that one roll.

"Would you like a drink?" she asked.

There were a pair of small circular wall lights on one side of the room and they cast the apartment into dusky shadow. I went over and sat on the arm of a big leather chair and stared out over the city. A faint hum like bees on a summer day came up, mingled with the subtle whiff of flowers, hot concrete and gasoline fumes. It hadn't exactly been my day but somehow I felt content.

I didn't move, neither did she switch on a light, but suddenly she was right beside me, one hand resting lightly on my shoulder as she passed me something long and cool in a long, cool glass.

"Cheers," she said, in the English way.

The drink tasted of limes and old bourbon. We sat looking at the dusk and the neon signs and the smog.

"Pretty, isn't it?" she said. She sounded quite serious.

"If you like that sort of thing," I said. The drink tasted good and I could have sat there all night, but I had to go to work.

I stood up to face her. She fidgeted and I couldn't see her expression very well. The room had gotten quite dark by now and she went over and put on a big standard lamp which knocked all hell out of the shadows.

"Come on, Miss Johnson," I said. "I've had quite a day. What can I do for you?"

"I'm sorry," she said. "It's rather difficult making a start."

"It usually is," I said. "People mainly employ P.I.s because they find it even more difficult explaining to the police."

"It's nothing like that," she said.

"It never is," I said gently. I was used to awkward clients beating a roundabout way to the truth, but this girl had some quality which got me guessing. But it would be difficult to help without knowing what was burning a hole in her pants. Though of course I didn't tell her that.

"What sort of investigator are you?" she asked.

"People usually send for me for their lousy jobs," I said. "They want old scores settled, facts best left buried dug up, vicious truths verified. You name them, I get them. All the brutal, dirty, lowdown, tough, mucky jobs that no one else will tackle. I don't come cheap but I do guarantee some sort of return."

Miss Johnson looked startled. "You sound rather bitter," she said.

"I didn't mean to," I replied, "but you asked what the score was. If you want level I carry a gun, rate fairly high marks for judo and can look out for myself in a roughhouse. But everything has to be square and above board. My L.A. licence was pretty hard to get and I'd like to hang on to it."

She nodded and got a cigarette out of a box on a long mahogany coffee table.

"About what I thought," she said. "I picked the right man."

"Now suppose we sit and get down to some serious conversation," I said.

A low laugh chased the shadows off her face. "I'm sorry," she said again. "I lost my brother about a year ago and I need help rather badly."

I studied my toecap assiduously. The old brother gag had been rather overworked this season.

"Before we begin, Miss Johnson," I said, "just why did you pick my name out of the *Examiner* like that? It was an awful small paragraph."

"Curiously enough," she said, "it had nothing to do with

you originally. What jumped out of the page at me was the name of Horvis. Horvis is a big name in Detroit."

I sat up. Neither of us said anything for a minute.

"Why should you be interested in the death of Horvis?" I said. "I know his brother is a big shot in Detroit but that seems to me highly incidental."

"There is a connection, Mr. Faraday. Of that I'm convinced."

Sherry Johnson's voice had drastically changed and I looked at her sharply. Her skin seemed to be tightly drawn around the eyes and she puffed nervously at her cigarette.

"I had a brother who was a brilliant engineer," she said. "Ralph was engaged first with General Motors in Detroit and then some while later he met Leslie Horvis. Leslie was in a much smaller way then and Ralph took over research in his design and production department and helped him build up his business; his future looked bright."

She stopped and looked fiercely out over the multi-coloured glare of the night sky.

"Everything went well until about two years ago. It was only gradually that I began to learn Ralph was working on something and it was worth a lot of money."

Her brother's invention was a fully automatic, electronically controlled set-up for car assembly lines that was one hundred per cent foolproof. It needed only about half a dozen men to run and would have been worth millions.

"Is it feasible?" I asked.

"Miss Johnson looked at me straight. "Not only feasible," she said. "Ralph had the problem licked. That's why he was killed."

This time I really sat up. "Go on."

"There would be millions in it, of course," she said. "Not only for the inventor but for the company or companies which controlled the line-up. And lots of people would be interested in its suppression. From rivals who might go to the wall to the thousands of motor workers made redundant."

"To say nothing of their union bosses," I said.

There was a silence again for a moment. A silence broken by, a long way off, the wail of an ambulance siren down in the city, under the neon and the stars. I sighed in the semi-gloom. It had been a long day and I was only at the beginning of the tangle.

"You still haven't told me about your brother," I reminded her. She went over and looked out of the window.

"He went out one night about a year ago," she said. "I didn't see him until about two days later. The police found him on an empty lot. He'd been shot and they never got the killer."

A trace of green still lingered in the evening sky. I'd gotten out my scratch pad to take some notes but it fell to the ground unnoticed.

"I'm sorry," I said.

"Don't be," she said. "It seems a long time ago now and it doesn't hurt any more."

Trying to make my voice sound casual, I asked, "How was your brother shot?"

"I believe the gun was a ·45," she said. "It was a close-range job, the police told me. His clothes were scorched and they said a silencer must have been used because the autopsy established that he'd been shot right in broad daylight, just behind a row of houses."

I felt a tingling along my nerve ends and went to join her at the window. I didn't know what the hell all this was about, why she had chosen me, whether the story she had just told me was phoney or real, but somehow the whole added up in a queer, crazy, distorted sort of way. The two Horvis brothers, the silenced gun, the three murders, two separated by nearly two thousand miles and a year in time. I'd once seen a film in which the camera was supposed to have seen the story through the eyes of a madman. I felt rather like that tonight.

"What made you come out here?" I asked.

"Don't you see, it can't be a coincidence," she said, turning to face me. "The deaths had to be linked; that's why I flew straight out."

"Why not leave all this to the police, Miss Johnson?" I asked. "That's what they're for. Anyway, why pick on me? I'm off the case—came way off when my client died."

"You needn't be," she said. "I have money."

"Here we go again," I said. "All right. Consider me engaged, but you may not like what I come up with."

"That's understood," she said. I had an insane idea that I was seeing the same picture around for the fourth time when she went to a satinwood table and started writing out a cheque. I went over and angrily studied the sky and the bloodshot neons. Something wasn't right—hadn't been right for a long while, and I was riled because I seemed to be picking up all the wrong ends. I unfolded the piece of paper she handed me. The cheque was made out for four hundred dollars. My stock was going down. Nevertheless, nice eating money. "I'll get you a receipt for this," I said.

I made arrangements to call her in a couple of days and got up to go. I finished my drink and went on over to the door.

"If I were you I wouldn't advertise your presence in L.A. or your business," I said. "Going to be here long?"

"As long as it takes," she said.

"Hope you won't be disappointed," I said.

In the corridor the heat was stifling, but the coolness of later evening was beginning to come on. The key was still giving confidence to my finger tips as I gum-shoed back to the apartment door. I listened for a long ten seconds but there was no stir. No scratch of a telephone dial or other unusual noise; like for instance a door opening in the apartment and a concealed eavesdropper coming out.

I shook my head. You have a nasty mind, Faraday, I told myself. All the same Miss Johnson, I'd like to believe you. I went on down in the lift. In the foyer I went in a booth and dialled. Admiral Dewey was bent double with unctious humility, earning a tip from a visiting senator and his wife. He made Uriah Heep look like a straight-shooting, clean-cut All-American. I heard assorted static for what seemed like half an hour and then Dan Tucker's boom. I told him all about my new client; his breath came out in a big poof when I mentioned Ralph Johnson.

He was shot with a silenced ·45, she thinks," I said. "Should be easy to check."

"I got MacNamara's report in front of me," he said. "Horvis was shot with a silenced ·45, the same gun that killed Braganza, ballistics say. That ain't conclusive, of course. We'll have to check with ballistics in Detroit, but things are beginning to move."

"Thanks, Dan," I said. "In the meantime I'd appreciate it if you'd leave the girl to me. I'll let you know if anything breaks."

"A deal," he said. "But if the D.A. starts getting any hotter under the collar he may put the whole thing at a higher level, in which case I can't help much."

I thanked him and hung up. I stared at the wall of the booth. Someone had scrawled a rude couplet on the front cover of the directory. I called Admiral Dewey over.

"Disgraceful. We don't expect this of the Bissell Building," I told him, wagging a forefinger.

His eyes popped. "Most unfortunate, sir. I'll have it removed right away."

"Very wise," I said. "Otherwise you might find yourself demoted to Post Captain."

I left him bawling out the hall porter and went on out. It was a beautiful night but I had no time to fool around with the skyline and the date palms. I went on over to the parking lot. The gold-plated Cadillac had gone but the Buick had plenty of company. The night was very quiet except for the chirping of crickets and I paused by the board fence before going on over to the car.

Someone lit a cigarette in one of the parked autos, there was a breath close to my face and something tore out a long sliver of board from the fence about two feet from where I stood. I went down and hit the dirt, rolling over and reaching for the butt of the Smith-Wesson all in one movement, as the small plop of the report reached me.

My nerves were screaming and I was calling myself bitterly all kinds of a fool, but I felt better as I eased back the safety catch. The click, small as it was, set something scuttering on the other side of the park. I saw a dark shape pass the rows of cars. I slid on my belly over towards the shadow of the Buick and as I felt gravel rasp under my hands I saw a figure momentarily silhouetted in front of a row of trash cans.

I chanced a shot, without much hope but just to boost my morale. It went wide, sending a garbage lid clattering with a great clang, but it put the seven bells of fear into my friend. He took the board fence in a rush and I heard feet receding into the distance. As I gained the sidewalk a car engine gunned behind me. I whirled just in time to see a tourer parked next to my Buick streak forward and pull out of the lot with a slurring of tyres.

It went off down the street pretty fast and I knew it would be no use following. My athletic friend would be aboard once he had gone a couple of blocks. My first instinct was to follow in my car but I had managed to keep going for some years with the aid of a certain native caution. Though I had made at least a dozen elementary mistakes today, reason and method were beginning to take over.

I replaced the garbage can lid and then went over the ground with my pencil flash looking for blood. There was none and it confirmed that I had missed him by a good yard. I decided not to bother Tucker again; it could do no good and my friends had my address anyway, if they wanted to come calling. I went over the Buick with the flash; I couldn't see if it had been tampered with but I decided to make sure. I went on back to the Bissell Building and bought a reel of twine from the kiosk in the foyer.

Admiral Dewey gave me a smart salutation from the other side of the lobby and pointed with pride to a new directory hanging up in the booth. I figured he must at least be a vice-president of the League of Decency. I went on out to the lot. It was deserted and I felt sure no one would be coming back

after our little shooting match. I fixed up a piece of twine
to the ignition and rove it through my side window to give a
side pull into the on position.

The other piece I tied round the starter switch on the dash
and trailed it straight back over the car body. About thirty
feet away I pulled cautiously on the first piece of twine. About
four years before an old chum of mine on the regular force,
one Barney Calleran had been blown to lace by a wired jalopy.
It was unlikely tonight but you never knew.

A moment's pause and then the reassuring green wink of
light from my dash. I had disengaged the gears and when I
pulled the second piece of twine there was a thunderous purr.
I let the engine idle for about half a minute and then walked
in. I gunned out of the lot and drove for home. There was a
cool wind coming up from the hills, which was welcome, and
though it wasn't yet midnight, traffic and lights were beginning to fade a little, like when the peak is past.

When I got home I drove the car into the entrance of the
lot and triggered the floodlights. The area blazed like daylight but there was nothing moving. I drove on into the car-
port; put the car hood up, went on in and locked up. I shut-
tered the windows, just in case, and made myself some coffee.
While I undressed I listened to the local radio bulletin but
there was nothing new on the Horvis killing; there was only
a brief two-line mention of it right at the end, just before the
baseball news.

I flipped the switch, killed the lounge lights and went on up.
In a corner of my bedroom was a little round Japanese inlaid
table that sometimes did duty as an impromptu telephone
stand or was pressed into use as a card table. It had small
drawers let into three front edges of its octangle. It seemed
just right for my purpose. It was too solid to knock over in the
ordinary way but just to make sure I jammed it up in an
angle of the room, where two walls gave it added support.
Underneath, it had deep panels of wood, which extended down
about four inches. I got a roll of sticky tape out of the kitchen
and up-ended the table as a start. After a minute I found a

deep crack in the underside of the table, right where two pieces of the panelling joined.

I slipped Mrs. Standish's key into this crack and then gummed the whole thing over with the black tape. It fitted snugly into the shadow cast inside the join and couldn't be seen, even under quite strong electric light. Then I turned the table the right way up, put the books back, doused the lights and went to bed. I slept badly for once.

I kept having dreams in which a nude Mrs. Standish was pursued by an oddly animated Mr. Horvis. He kept saying, "Most amusing, Mr. Faraday," and every now and again there was a popping noise which kept me twitching, even in my sleep. I awoke sweating at dawn.

A bird was practising scales for the Met outside my window and plenty of light was spilling through the shutters. I turned over again and this time I slept well.

5

Captain Jacoby

I WAS AWAKENED by a loud hammering on the porch door. I shook the sleep from my eyes and went on down. It was only just gone half after seven. I looked through the gauze curtains on to the porch. Two big men in dark suits stood there admiring the view. They had cop written all over them. They obviously weren't going away, so I opened up.

"Take your time," one of them said sourly. He looked nasty.

"Sure," I said. "Had a bath and a sandwich on the way down."

The bigger one said nothing but his eyes smouldered. He started to get out a badge in a leather billfold. I stopped him.

"All right," I said. "Don't let's play games. What's the trouble?"

I had recognized the younger one as a junior detective called McGiver. He looked embarrassed.

"Mind if we come in?" said the big cop. His voice was deceptively mild but I recognized the type. As a beat man he had probably worked his old mother over with a night stick during the evenings just to keep his hand in.

"You got a warrant?" I asked. A red spot came and went on his cheek.

"No," he said slowly. "But we can get one if you feel that way about it."

"Don't bother," I said. "Come on in. I hate lying around the sack in the morning, anyway."

He let that ride. The younger one went first and he waited to follow me into the living-room. "Just a friendly visit," he said unconvincingly.

I went over to the table and lit a cigarette. "What can I do for you boys?" I asked.

"We ask the questions, shamus," said the big cop. He looked round the room like the furnishings offended his eyes.

"Nice layout you got here."

"Yeah," I said. "You get some ritzy gifts from cigarette coupons these days."

The young cop said nothing but went and stood near the door. His eyes flashed a warning at me.

The big cop snorted. "Captain Jacoby wants a word with you."

"Horvis?" I said.

"That, and some other," he said.

"I already spoke my piece," I said.

"I don't hear you so well," said the big cop. "Captain Jacoby ain't seen you. We're City Force."

"Nice for you," I said.

The big cop cleared his throat. Then he spat. The gob went on to my white Persian carpet and lay here. The big cop grinned.

"Sorry about that," he said.

I went round the coffee table fast but stopped. The young cop moved over from the door and his eyes spelt a clear signal. I looked the big cop in the face.

"Any more of that, fatso, and you go out of the door on your ear, badge or no badge," I said evenly.

He smiled a dead smile in his pasty face. "Why do they always have to be so tough?" he asked McGiver. I caught the flash of a brass knuckle as he put it back in his pocket. He went around the table and ground the carpet with his heel.

"That better, shamus?" he asked. I didn't answer but went on upstairs and dressed. McGiver came up after me and sat outside the door. When I had finished I put some coffee on and took my time over breakfast. When I went back into the living-room the big cop had his mouth set like a rat trap.

"We ain't got all day," he said sullenly.

"No hurry," I told him. We went out. I got in the front seat of the black prowl car next to the fat boy. McGiver sat in back. The big man gave her the gun. He drove flat out all the way, with the siren going full blast. We pulled up in front of a dirty brownstone building that housed the downtown police headquarters. The big boy took about half a pound of rubber off the tyres as he put the brake on.

"Out," he grunted. I got out and walked between the two of them up a flight of dirty steps and into a drab reception office that looked like a set out of an Algerian movie. A B picture at that.

A cop in a shabby-looking uniform sat at a table littered with peanut shucks; he had his elbows on the desk and was reading a magazine. He wore no tie and looked as if he hadn't shaved; he never got up nor shifted the gum in his mouth as we went by. Some force.

"Smart lay-out," I said.

"Can't afford polish on our money, shamus," said the big guy.

Someone snickered. We went along a corridor, just as shabby and dirty as the first room. The big cop went through a glass-topped door which had DETECTIVES stencilled on it. The young one followed me in. We were in a small room painted in cream and brown. A water fountain with a tray of paper cups stood in one corner; some dusty filing cabinets, brown regulation benches, a table or two, a few chairs. The ceiling fan wasn't working. On the walls a few fly-blown notices stared back. The paint was flaking. Underfoot the linoleum was cracked and split; there were cigarette ends and the shucks of peanuts.

"You wouldn't get a seal from Good Housekeeping," I said.

The big cop scowled and McGiver cracked me a smile. He looked friendly.

"Wait here," the big guy said and went out through a door

labelled CAPTAIN OF DETECTIVES. I took the weight off my feet.
I blinked at a police notice.

"Nice friends you got," I told McGiver. He shifted uneasily.
"You know what these big men are."

"The only thing big about him is his belly," I told him.

We sat for about fifteen minutes and then the door opened
again. The big cop beckoned me. I went on over and McGiver
followed. We were in a smaller room. It was still the same
crummy décor but with a bit more opulence if you know what
I mean. There were some bright lights hanging from the ceiling, green-shaded desk lamps more files and office furniture.
Behind an acre of desk stuck down in the middle of a grey
rug sat Captain Jacoby. He was a short man with enormously
broad shoulders.

His head was almost bald and from either side his rocky
skull projected two jug-like ears. He had hands like boulders
and they sparkled with cheap rings. He wore a quiet-looking
blue suit and under the desk I could see he wore black shoes
with built-up heels. Some bozo.

He was a remarkable sight. He said nothing but motioned
me to a swivel chair in front of him. McGiver stood near the
door and the big officer sat on a corner of the desk. Captain
Jacoby's face was bisected by a thin black mustache which
ran mathematically straight between his nose and upper lip.
He had two gold teeth too, but that was the only gilded thing
about him.

"Guess we'll have to wipe this guy's ass for him," he said to
the wallpaper.

"I don't think we're going to get on, Captain," I said.

He looked at me sharply and the big man's jaw sagged a
couple of millimetres; he shifted on the corner of the desk.

"Like I said," he said hoarsely. "He's sassy."

"Shut up," Jacoby almost screamed at him. He turned un-
naturally brilliant eyes towards me and eyed me for a long
minute.

"Carry a gun," he said, without looking up.

"Sometimes," I said.

"What does that mean?" he said, still in the same deceptively mild voice. His hands were folded primly on the desk. I saw hands like that once on a Polish coal-miner who was convicted of killing his wife by manual strangulation. Jacoby's hands looked like two piles of rock sitting on the blotter.

"Like I said," I told him. "I left it home today."

The big man moved in behind me and went over my inner pockets. He made a poor job of it. He would have missed a tommy gun with that technique.

"You got a gun licence?" said Jacoby. He sat immobile, his eyes unblinking. This was the big deal. The S.S. stuff that was supposed to crack the suspect's morale. I put down my gun licence and sat back trading him glance for glance. After a bit he got tired of the Pelmanism and looked away.

"Let's quit pooping around," I told him. "What do you want, Captain?"

The fat cop sucked in his breath. Jacoby sat bolt upright and if he had any hair it would have bristled. His scalp seemed to ripple.

"I want a complete rundown, shamus," he said. "Everything you know about the Horvis killing. . . ."

"We've been all over that," I said. "Get Captain Tucker in."

"It's Tucker's day off, shamus," he said with a sneer. "He's gone fishing. You're talking to me."

"Get the file out and stop wasting my time," I told him.

"This is a different department," Jacoby said and the big cop sniggered.

"You know my legal rights as well as I do," I said. "Save all this corny Gestapo stuff for the teenage junkies. Rubber truncheons went out with silent films."

I hit home there. The room went quiet and Jacoby a shade of yellow white. He tortured his face into a smile.

"Want to call your lawyer?" He held out his hand to the telephone.

"No thanks," I said. "It wouldn't get any farther than the switchboard. What are you after, Captain? Someone put the finger on you?"

He got up then and came round the desk. He was only a little man but he seemed as broad as a motor boat. I sat where I was. He pushed his face up against mine and I could catch the stench of stale breath and garlic. It was pretty strong.

"You'll never keep friends unless you use the right tooth-paste," I told him. "To preserve your P.R. image you should mug up on the sanitary angle."

His cold eyes never left mine. "For the last time, shamus," he breathed. "Are you going to open up?"

I opened my mouth to make with the verbiage when his big hand came up, fist clenched and heavy with rings, and caught me a solid thump on the side of the head. Pain lanced way up to the top of my skull and the room rocked. I tasted blood and the big detective tittered.

"Why is it you little men always have to try throwing your weight about?" I said and stood up quickly. His second blow caught me on the shoulder and momentarily spun me off balance. Nobody moved and the air in the office was heavy with expectation. I spat blood out on Jacoby's carpet.

I looked at him steadily. "Try that once more and I'll rip your nostrils out, whether it affects my licence or not," I told him. For the first time I saw fear in his face, quickly overlaid with rage. I had overstepped the mark this time. From now on I had to play by ear.

Jacoby grunted and swung at me, his fist balled for a knockout blow. I moved in behind, caught him and then found the right arm lock. He grunted again, this time in pain as I put on the pressure and his revolver fell down with a loud clatter on the floor. McGiver hadn't moved but then I felt a burning pain in the back. The big cop was standing behind me, his boot poised for another kick. I twisted Jacoby round and heeled fat belly once, twice and again in the groin. He moaned and fell forward, his head striking the desk. I had been fond of that carpet.

I must have got a bit mad then, for I felt Jacoby's arm bones begin to crack. He turned white and a low moaning noise came out from between his teeth. Saliva started running down his shirt front.

"Now, Captain," I gritted, "you were saying. . . ."

Then, and only then, did McGiver move over from his place by the door.

"All right, Faraday," he said sharply. "That's enough."

"Sure," I said, all my rage dissipated. "I was only showing the captain one or two elementary holds."

Jacoby half fell into his swivel chair and rested his head on the desk.

"Just for the record, Captain," McGiver told Jacoby in a loud, clear voice, "I saw you and Mullins hit the detainee first. This is clearly a breach of regulations. I think it would be best if the whole question of charges was dropped for the good of the force."

Jacoby looked up; his face was a mask of hatred.

"Go on, McGiver," he said at last in a thick voice.

"I just wanted to make my own position clear, Captain," McGiver said. "In the event of any public proceedings I should have to make my views clear and they would support Mr. Faraday one hundred per cent as to what happened here today."

Jacoby nodded slowly. Sweat shone on his bald head.

Mullins started to stir on the floor. Presently he sat up and began to retch quietly.

"For Christ's sake get him out of here," said Jacoby in disgust. "I'm not due a new carpet until next year's appropriations."

"Well, Captain," said McGiver after a long minute. "No charges?"

Jacoby looked at Mullins with contempt. "No charges," he said at last and turned away. McGiver helped Mullins to a chair. As he straightened up he looked at me and his right eye quivered a fraction.

"Where were we?" I said.

Jacoby choked. "Get him out of here," he gritted. "A night in the tank will cool him down."

I went past Mullins and stood in front of Jacoby. I picked

up my documents and slowly put them back in my pocket. He made no move to stop me.

"Thank you, Captain," I said. "I think we understand one another now."

"Get out," he said thickly.

"Certainly, Captain," I said. "The air is a little oppressive in here. I'll be seeing you."

He gave me a long look that was like acid. "That's one thing you can be sure of, shamus," he said, with something like his old manner. I stepped over Mullins's feet and went on out with McGiver. In the corridor the air seemed fresher, though the heat had started again.

"Thanks," I told McGiver.

"Forget it," he said. "He had it coming for a long time."

We walked on down the corridor to the desk in the outer office.

"Sorry, I'll have to book you," he said. "I'll see what I can do in the morning. You want a lawyer?"

I shook my head. We went over to the desk. The cop put down his magazine and fished for a piece of popcorn in a tooth cavity.

"Meet Michael Faraday," said McGiver. "He just bopped Captain Jacoby."

The cop sat up. He looked at me with respect. "The hell he did. Put it there," he said and held out his hand.

"A police officer is always loyal to his colleagues," said McGiver dryly.

I put down all my documents and private papers on the desk and the cop entered them in a book and put them away in an old green safe. McGiver let me keep my matches and then handed me over to the turnkey, a morose cop of about fifty with sandy hair. He took me to a little concrete cell enclosed with heavy iron grilles. There were two bunks, a toilet which stank and a tiled washbasin. A grey-haired drunk sprawled on one of the bunks sleeping it off.

The air was stifling hot. The first thing I did was flush the latrine which cleared the atmosphere a bit. There was a small

piece of mirror screwed to the wall by the washbasin. I looked
a mess. One side of my head was caked with blood, my clothes
were rumpled. Blood was still filling my mouth, I had a splitting headache and my back was beginning to give out Morse
signals where Mullins had kicked me. I had a wash and took
some of the blood off my face.

Then I rinsed my mouth and felt better. I felt something
move against my tongue and found a small piece of tooth was
breaking off. I washed the fragment, found an old envelope
in an inner pocket of my jacket, carefully wrapped the sliver
in it and put it back in my pocket. I took off my jacket and
sat down on a bunk as far away from the drunk's snores as
possible. Pretty soon my eyelids closed in the stifling heat and
despite the throbbing in my jaws I dozed.

2

When I woke it was around noon. The drunk was still asleep
and whistling Beethoven's Ninth through his nostrils. It was
hotter than ever and I went over to the washbasin and sluiced
myself. That made me feel worse. The hum of traffic came
up from the boulevard. There was a clank in the corridor
and the turnkey appeared. He put down a tray on my bunk.

"Special today," he said. "Irish stew and mash. Okay?"

"Swell," I said insincerely. "How about R.V.W.?"

"Solids are murder to him," he said. "We don't want to
spoil his digestion."

He moved off down the corridor. I viewed the mess on the
plate with distaste. The heat and the stench in the cells made
up my mind; I took the platter over near the door but three
or four mouthfuls was enough. I saved the bread for later,
but the coffee was welcome. Presently there was another clatter
at the door and McGiver came in. He whistled when he saw
my face.

"Jeezechrise," he said. I gave him Stella's name and number
and he promised to call her in the afternoon. He went on out,
the door shut behind him and the station settled down to its

afternoon torpor. I sat back on my bunk and leaned against the wall. I must have slept again. The next thing I remember was the toilet being used and then something that looked like an old bundle of clothes standing in front of me. It was the occupant of the other bunk.

"My name's Jarvis," he said, holding out a claw-like hand. I tried to shake it but with his D.T.s and all, it was quite a job. "Horse Jarvis," he added, making unsteadily for his bunk. He sat down clumsily, almost falling off the edge of the iron framing. His eyes were yellow and his long, sad face had all the typical signs of the far-gone alcoholic. He rambled on for a minute or two and then his blurred eyes seemed to clear. "God a' Heaven," he said. "Whaddya done to your face?" I told him. He clapped his hands and chuckled. "That Jacoby's a mean bastard. Real mean. I had a cousin in this tank once. He run up against that Jacoby. For nothin' at all! Lost most of his teeth all acrost one side of his face."

He seriously examined the cement wall of the cell. "For nothin' at all," he breathed quietly, more to himself than to me. I patted the pocket where the fragment of my tooth was resting. Horse Jarvis got down slowly on his bunk again; he put his hands under his head, which he cradled like a child and was soon sleeping the blissful dreams of the alcoholic.

The sun sank, a fiery ball over L.A. and I kept getting the petrol fumes and flowers and the swish of the home-going traffic. I looked at my watch. It was already around seven. That is, if it hadn't stopped. I re-wound it absently and went over to look at myself again. I felt a little better and the head looked better too, though it was still a symphony in blue and red. I bathed my face again.

When I came away from the washbasin a bulb in the ceiling suddenly came alight. It was so dim it made the cell seem darker. I sat down. There was nothing else to do and I couldn't see to read my paper, even if I had felt like it. About eight the turnkey came around. He brought minced beef, some watery cabbage, a thin slice of blueberry pie and more institutional coffee.

This time the drunk took some coffee. It made him cough

and seemed to start up something in his stomach. At any rate he seemed to be awake half the night. The turnkey went off, rattling his keys. At the door he turned and said in a brisk, breezy voice, "Anything else room service can do for you gentlemen, before we close down for the night?"

I shook my head.

"Hilton Hotel," the drunk grunted emotionlessly from out of the back of his head, half buried in a blanket. The turnkey went off unblinkingly, soullessly efficient, wishing us a pleasant evening. I loosened my tie and got ready for bed. The daylight died and soon it was dark outside. The noise of the traffic went on. Just before ten a stout cop with a black mustache looked in through the grille, nodded with a touch of condescension like he had a good supper in the next room and was free to wander about. He went off presently, singing "Sweet Adeline" to himself in a tuneless voice. There was a lot of thin whistling in the distance, metal doors opening and closing, footsteps, the clatter of tin slop bowls.

"Chrissake buddy, wrap it up," yelled the drunk to nobody in particular. "More like Bethlehem Steel in here."

Soon after, the noise died away and the dim bulb in the ceiling went out. Outside, in the corridor, a tiny red lamp cast a garish glow. The draught sucked in heavily through the grille, over the concrete floor, stale with cigarette smoke, carbolic soap and yesterday's stew. Great. The day's entertainment was over. I rolled myself in the blankets and fell asleep. As an evening out I preferred the night before.

3

It was dawn. My mouth tasted full of potato peelings and old string vests. The time was just after six but already the sound of buckets and brooms came along the antiseptic concrete corridor. I got up and sat on the edge of the bunk. My friend was still asleep. Beams of sunlight came in at the window and knocked hell out of the dust. My head felt a whole lot better.

I went to the washbasin and to my surprise hot water came out. I sponged my face. The swelling was going down and the inside of my mouth felt as though it was attached to the outside. I couldn't do much about the stubble on my chin, but I managed to comb my hair so as to hide most of the damage. Then I finished my cigarette, put my jacket back on, knotted up my tie and got ready for the day. I felt I might live with a little food and kindness.

It was now just coming up to seven. The original flunkey was back, making with the bright aphorisms. His tray even smelt good. The drunk slept on but I managed some toast, some bacon and a couple of cups of coffee. I could have done with more but I left half in the chipped tin jug for the old guy. The breakfast even began to taste good. Jeeze, Mike, I told myself; better watch it. You're getting used to the penal system.

I sat on the bunk, smoked another cigarette and read the day-old paper. Around eight there was a lot of coming and going and presently a rumpus in the corridor. Outside, cars backed and snarled and exhaust smoke curled in at the window. The old drunk coughed and then sat up. He drank his coffee without opening his eyes, feeling for the pot and his mug like a blind man. Then he lay down again and went to sleep.

I went over near the door and amused myself by trying to see across the corridor into the main office; the door was half ajar. Presently someone left it open all the way. A familiar figure in a dark suit went across. It was the big cop, the one I'd laid out. He didn't look in my direction but went on out. I heard his car gun into the distance. Then Jacoby went by, walking on the balls of his feet, hunched to one side, his head turned away at an angle.

"Good morning, Captain," I called cheerily. He didn't answer or cease his measured pace, but his arms, straight at the side, tensed, and his fists balled. He went on out, still walking like that. Impressive stuff, mighty tough. Real Warner Brothers. I was laughing as I turned back and set my cigarette-end spinning through the window into the yard. There was a clang at the door and Dan Tucker was standing in the entrance. His huge bulk seemed to fill the cell. His pink face looked worried and his jaw was set. There was a curious carmine flush all around his neck and I guessed he had just been with Jacoby.

"Outside, mister," said the turnkey. "Hope we made you comfortable."

"No hard feelings," I said. I went over to the old guy and pushed a packet of Camels under the rolled blanket that served him as a pillow.

In the general office I checked my wallet and papers; my P.I. licence among them. Nothing missing. I signed a chit for their receipt and put my stuff away.

"We'll go get a bite," said Dan. We went out and down the front steps. The sun hit me like a baseball bat. It felt antiseptic on my face. We stopped on the pavement to let the traffic go by. Tucker grabbed my arm and his eyes looked angry.

"Sorry I was away," he said heavily.

"Not your fault," I said. "How was the fishing?"

"Never mind that," he said. "Christ! Faraday, I thought you had more sense. I've had quite an hour in there. Did you have to hit him?" He almost yelled the last words.

"Sorry, Dan," I said. "I didn't have much choice. It was either that or get my physique re-arranged by him and his S.S. pal. I appreciate what you did and, believe me, I'm grateful."

He looked at me soberly and the anger had died out of his eyes.

"You know you could have lost your licence?"

I nodded. "I had McGiver go to bat for me. He's the only one in step in that Keystone set-up."

Tucker's face seemed to be going through a number of emotions, and finally he grinned. "What in hell did you do to him?" he asked. "He was sitting like someone tried to give his ass the hot foot."

"Fair exchange," I said. I showed him the side of my face. He whistled and dodged round a passer-by with an agility that belied his size.

"See what you mean," he said, "but take it easy in future."

We crossed over the road to a lunch counter almost opposite. The place was fairly full but in back the crowd thinned out and we found a spot in a corner and pulled up two stools.

"What's the set-up, Dan?" I asked. "What were those two clowns after?"

Tucker shrugged. "It's a cock-eyed army," he said. He studied the menu the hash-slinger brought us. He was a consumptive-looking youth with a prominent neck structure. Tucker ordered beefburgers, coffee, a flapjack with syrup and cream.

"Want the same?" he asked.

"For God's sake," I said. "For breakfast?"

"Breakfast, dinner, lunch, suppertime, any old time," he said. "What the hell does it matter so long as you got a good gut."

"What about the apples?" I said.

"Bought some on the way down," he answered. "Got 'em out in the car."

I gave up and ordered black coffee and toast. The youth brought back two chunks of bread. Sandwiched in between was something which looked like old motor tyres. A nauseous miasma came up from the plate.

"Have you got a licence for those?" I asked the youth. He looked bewildered.

"Something wrong?" He havered on one foot.

"Delicious!" bellowed Dan Tucker as he smeared the abortion with a half-gallon bucket of mustard. I shut up and drank my coffee. "We're doing well," he said between mouthfuls.

"You've arrested someone, then," I said.

"Don't be funny," he snapped. "We're making progress— for this case."

"All right," I said. "I'll buy it. You found out Adrian Horvis takes size eight and a half in hats. The Filipino houseboy——"

"Look," said Tucker, his voice indistinct through tortured beef. "If you don't want to hear. . . ."

I opened up my ears.

"We came up with something," he said. "The whole set-up begins to fit. The riflings on the bullets taken from the Johnson lad in Detroit and from Braganza and Horvis in L.A. match up perfectly in every characteristic. There's no doubt about it. The same gun was used in each case."

He wrinkled his brows. "In the transcript of inquiries a woman in Detroit said she saw a man hanging about the lot where the Johnson boy was killed. Curious. This woman said he was a young man—only he had white hair. Leastways, she said he had a young face. But nothing ever came of it."

"Big lead," I said.

"Can you do any better?" he said.

"You got me there," I said. "Any more news on the P.M.?"

"Nothing that could help," said Tucker. "Horvis wasn't in exactly A.1. condition but he couldn't have lived, even after one shot. Whoever killed him knew his job. The bullet had been cut to spread out and make a big hole."

"Nice," I said. The sun was spilling in at the door of the lunch counter and making patterns on the tiled floor. I finished off my coffee. It knocked all hell out of the inside of my mouth where it was raw around my cracked tooth, but I felt better. The wheels of my brain were moving now, slowly for sure, but they were moving, nevertheless.

"You were going to drive me home, of course?" I said.

"Why not?" he said. "It's a legitimate public expense. And it's not every day a P.I. takes a poke at a cop and gets away with it."

I grinned. Tucker called for the check, paid it with a grimace and we went out. The sun was hotting up. Tucker climbed into the driving seat of a black prowl car. He waved away an attendant cop, and I slid in beside him on the front seat. Dan Tucker pulled out quietly; he drove unostentatiously and well. He didn't use the siren. I felt tired again and my head began to ache. Tucker took an apple out of a package in the dash cubby and began to crunch it. I closed my eyes then, but the sharp sound still irritated.

"I presume we're still working together?" I said.

"Yeah," he said, crossing a light junction at the red. A cop blew a whistle and then tore off a belated salute as he recognized the car.

"By law you're supposed to tell me everything you know," he said. "That's a citizen's duty. And I might, if I'm feeling in the right mood, feed you a little information now and then."

"Sounds fair," I said. "I'd better invest in a couple of pounds of apples to keep your digestion sweet."

He chuckled and tooled the big car up into Park West. "You live well for a P.I.," he said. "I thought all you boys earned hamburger money looking through wardrobe keyholes in motels."

"That was in the twenties," I said. "All the crooks are in the police these days. The victimized citizen rushes straight up to the muscular, clean-limbed P.I. and starts shedding greenbacks. It's a form of insurance."

"Is that what it is?" said Tucker. He laughed softly as he changed the gear and looked inquiringly at me. We slid up the driveway. The Buick was still in the car-port, collecting dew and dust from the street on the upholstery. The front door of the house was standing ajar. Tucker and I exchanged a glance. We walked up to the porch. Inside the living-room furniture was thrown down, pictures smashed, furniture covers ripped. Documents and papers were strewn over the floors. Dan Tucker went and leaned against a wall and pushed his hat on to the back of his head.

"I didn't hear no hurricane report," he said.

I went into the kitchen and the other rooms. Everywhere it was the same. I went back into the living-room.

"They left the roof," Tucker grunted.

"They're coming back for that tomorrow," I told him.

He moved over to the phone. "You want to make this official?"

"I'm a citizen aren't I?"

While he was on the phone I went on upstairs. The damage was less here; nevertheless, a crude old job. The table had been moved from its place but not turned over. I pushed it back and felt under with my fingers. The key was still there. A bunch of amateurs. I went down the stairs with almost a light step. In the kitchen I found a bottle of bourbon and some glasses. I got some ice cubes out of the Frigidaire and carried the lot into the living-room. I righted the coffee table and put down the bottle and glasses. Tucker was still on the phone. He was reversing the charges. I found some soda and made two long drinks with plenty of ice. Dan Tucker came off the phone and sat down heavily in a chair opposite me. He picked up his glass.

"Good luck," he said.

"I bet you're a riot at the police smoker," I said.

"The boys are on their way," he said. He put down his glass again. "I should have staked out someone here to keep an eye on the place."

"You didn't know," I reminded him. "You'd gone fishing."

"Yeah, that's right. Any idea what they might be after?"

I shrugged. "You don't think Jacoby. . . ." I started to say.

He almost exploded. He waved a thick finger at me. "Good God, no. He's only got another five years to go for a pension. Why in hell would he risk that?"

"All right," I said. "Just an idea. It was something funny Mrs. Standish said. Something about bad cops and things being lost in pigeon holes."

"Don't mean to say he took an axe to your sideboard," he said.

" 'Sides, whoever came here was looking for something. They wouldn't re-arrange the house just for a few bruised ribs. Don't make sense. It may be Keystone down in that precinct but that don't make it Huey Long country."

He sighed heavily and picked up his drink again.

"You proved your point," I said.

We sat and looked silently at the wreckage. It looked only slightly better than the San Francisco earthquake. Except that the décor was more up to date.

The thin wail of sirens began to split the air along Park West. They sounded very loud in the bright sunlight.

6

Mandy Mellow

I SAT IN THE KITCHEN and talked to McGiver. In the rest of the house there was the tramping of heavy feet. Finger-print men went round dusting, flashbulbs popped. Dan Tucker sat in the living room and decimated the apple population. I grinned at McGiver.

"You keep in the centre of things," he said.

"I try," I said. "Any news from Stella?"

"Sorry," he said, "I forgot. She wasn't at all surprised that she hadn't heard from you. But she seemed anxious." He hesitated. "She's a nice girl."

I said nothing. He shifted his feet on the tiled floor and fooled with his coffee cup.

"She asked you to give her a ring this evening if possible. Appears she's got some messages."

I nodded. McGiver cast a glance over his shoulder towards the open door. Shadowy figures passed, bearing one of my bureaus. It was a real circus.

"What's all this about?" he asked. "Dan doesn't usually go to town on a thing like this. Why the three-star treatment?"

I shrugged. "Hadn't you better ask Tucker? I'm still a number one suspect, according to Jacoby."

He grinned. "O.K. Call me nosy."

He finished his cup and stood up. We both strolled to the

door. Dan Tucker sat in the middle of chaos, his teeth wrapping round the remains of another apple. A group of detectives surrounded him, like acolytes with a high priest. He looked contented; this was his work. At the door there were two uniformed men and outside, a gaggle of police cars in the drive. It looked like Saturday Night Crime Club on T.V. Tucker beckoned me.

"Show over?" I asked.

"Nearly," he grunted. "Don't look as though we shall get much farther here."

"Prints?"

"Nary a useable one. Looks like whoever did this used thin rubber gloves."

"Careful fellas," I said.

"Like the rest of this case," he said. "I should start getting suspicious if we got leads. I'm not used to them."

"You'd be spoiled on an open-and-shut murder," I told him.

"If you don't mind I'll go and get some shut-eye," I said. "I'll clean up later."

"Right," he said. "We're all finished here anyway. I'll leave a couple of men on day and night, just in case. Give me a call tomorrow morning and we'll go over everything. See what the next move will be. And you'd better get back and report to the Johnson woman. Otherwise she may get impatient and pull out."

I nodded. I went upstairs and got a spare key for the kitchen door and gave it to Tucker for the men, so that they could brew themselves some coffee. A locksmith Tucker had called up from L.A. came in with a boy and started getting out his tools. He looked at the wreck of the front door and scratched his head. Then he went over and looked in the living-room.

"You got cops like some people got mice," he said.

I thanked him and went on upstairs. I set the alarm for mid-afternoon and then hit the sack. I heard the sirens when the prowl cars went away but after that I was dead to the world.

2

When the alarm rang it took me a long time to come around. It was like struggling up through layers of cream cheese. But I surfaced and looked at the clock. It was around four in the afternoon. Great slabs of sun came in the window and spread over the floor. The window was open and the sound of a mower came up. Outside, on a tree branch a blackbird came and sang Schubert. It sure was peaceful. I rolled over and incinerated a cigarette. My mouth and head felt a whole lot better; I lay on my back, smoked and looked at the ceiling. I could use a wodge of peace right now.

From below came the comforting sound of two large men talking, and the shifting of furniture. There seemed to be some controversy over baseball scores. I got up and went to the window. The street was quiet and the man with the mower was going indoors, carrying the grass box under his arm. A solitary black police car stood in my drive. All was right with the world.

I went in the bathroom and took a shower. I decided that I might live another twenty years, with care. I came back into the bedroom, tidied the mussed sheets and struggled into a clean shirt and my trousers. Then I got the office on the bedroom phone.

After a moment the receiver was lifted. It was a man's voice. For a moment I had a dry throat and it wasn't the cigarette. It was Bert Dexter.

"Oh, hullo Mike," he said. "Stella? She just stepped out for a couple of minutes. I'm taking the calls. Just a moment, she left some names on a pad. Someone called Snagge, a man named McGiver, a Miss Johnson."

"O.K. Bert, thanks," I said . "I know about most of them. Ask Stella to give me a ring when she comes in, will you?"

I rang off and put my shoes and socks on. I was just knotting my tie when there was a rap on the door. A big cop stood there. He was Irish, tough but friendly.

"All right, Mr. Faraday?" he asked. "Thought you might like a cup of coffee?"

"Thanks," I said. "I'll come on down."

In the kitchen the other cop, an older man with greying hair was sitting in my breakfast nook. He got up awkwardly but I told him to sit down again. The coffee was good. The Irishman had made it properly. He'd ground up the beans real fine.

In the living-room the place had been cleaned up. The furniture was all back, the pictures straightened, chairs righted, papers and books replaced on shelves and tables. I went over to the front door with my coffee cup. There was a new lock; it looked strong and efficient. I kicked a few wood shavings off the porch.

On the outside of the door two keys in a plastic bag were fixed to the wood with sticky tape; there was a bill stuck on the door too.

I rang Stella and told her I'd be in at the office in half an hour. When I had dressed and was ready for off, I made sure none of the sentries were about and went to the cupboard where I kept my guns. Curiously, nothing in this room had been disturbed. Anyway, my gun rack was intact. I broke out my favourite Smith-Wesson, put a couple of extra clips in the holster pouch and felt fully dressed. I went down to the living-room. The cops looked at me.

"No tail?" I said.

"Our instructions were to keep an eye on the house," said the Irishman.

"Make yourselves at home," I told them. I got in the car and drove off downtown. At the first intersection an aggressively polished scarlet Jaguar, one of those little English sports jobs bored across, chopping the air just in front of my bumper. The driver, a young fellow in a yellow sweater gave me a triumphant fanfare. He probably thought he was a good driver.

I pulled up in front of my block and went on up to the office. Bert Dexter had gone out and Stella was alone. She winced when she saw my face and made a big bustle with the coffee cups. I sat down behind the big desk. It seemed like a long time since I had been there. Stella put the coffee cup down on the blotter in front of me. She stuck two cigarettes in her mouth and lit them. Then she gave me one, sat down beside me and stirred her coffee. "Well?" she asked. Stella was great on the understatement. I told her. I filled in the whole story from the time I had left her two days before, to this morning. Leaving out the sexy bits, of course. Stella was a bit possessive for that. She bit her lip as I went on. For a minute there was silence and we sat drinking our coffee. The same spider, or perhaps its brother, performed acrobatics on a corner of the ceiling near the window blind. It didn't seem much cooler in the office and the air conditioning was still giving trouble.

"What are you thinking?" I asked. She wrinkled her nose.

"That you're a funny sort of a guy. You find your client murdered, get shot at, beaten up and slung into jail, all within forty-eight hours. Yet here you are, with another client and another retainer, bouncing up, all ready to be shot at or beaten up once again. Same old merry-go-round."

She laughed in a cynical sort of way and went to get some more coffee. I watched her go, appraising her wiggle expertly.

"I didn't know you cared," I said.

"It's not that," she said. "It's knowing that we're still in business and that I'm going to get paid regularly."

I put my head against her face and kissed a small curl that wandered over her forehead. She smelt cool and fresh, just like one of those deodorant ads. Except that they weren't so sexy with it.

"What's that for?" she said, all wide-eyed and surprised.

"For being so understanding," I said. "Which reminds me. . . ."

I took my cheque book out. I wrote her a cheque for a hundred dollars and tried to slip it in the vee of her sweater. She expertly intercepted my hand and took the slip of paper.

"What's this for?"

"A small bonus," I said. "For being Stella, and a few other things."

"You'll be spoiling me," she said. She got out her handbag and put the cheque away.

"I've got three calls," she said.

"I know," I said. "Bert told me. I've already seen McGiver. That leaves Charlie Snagge and Sherry Johnson. I've got to see her today. Any idea what Charlie wants?"

"He spoke of remembering something that might be helpful. Other than that, he wouldn't say."

Stella made a note or two and then sat tapping her teeth with a pencil.

"I think it would be a good idea if you saw Leslie Horvis and had a talk with him," she said. "He's in L.A. isn't he?"

I sat and blinked for a minute. I clean forgot about that aspect of the case, what with my night in jail and all.

"I should have made that cheque out for a bigger amount," I said.

She opened her handbag. "There's still time," she said.

I ignored her remark and sat on for a moment or two longer.

"What are you going to do about the key?" she said.

"I think I ought to work the old registered packet trick," I said. She made a note on that. The girl had real efficiency. Then she called Dan Tucker at home.

"Thought you wouldn't be asleep for long," he snorted.

I arranged to drop in at eleven the next morning when Horvis was coming to see him.

"The Johnson girl's still at the hotel," he said. "But she's not using the phone at all. Pretty cagey."

"I thought you weren't keeping her under observation," I said.

"Well, not so's you'd notice," he said. 'We did get one good picture though—with a telephoto. I'm having that wired to Detroit to see if it rings a bell."

I chuckled. "And they say the L.A. police are dumb," I said.

"Who says?" he wanted to know. I thanked him and rang off.

Then I got Stella to ring the Bissell Building. Sherry Johnson was home. She sounded surprised. "Where have you been?" she asked. "I expected a call yesterday."

"In jail," I said. I interrupted her questions. "Listen, Miss Johnson, I think we ought to have another talk. Will this evening do?"

She hesitated a minute. "Make it after ten."

"Thanks," I said. There hadn't been any frost on the wire but she hadn't exactly greeted me with the warmth of the old home fire.

Just then the phone rang. I took the call.

"Mr. Faraday?" The voice was deep and self-assured.

"Speaking."

"My name's Mandy Mellow. I run the Jazz Inn out on the edge of town."

I won the golliwog straight off. He was a big-time gambler who owned the Inn and interests in a couple of dozen other joints besides. Strictly straight as far as I knew, but not a man to fool with. Some people around town called him Marsh Mellow, but they didn't know him. He wasn't soft at all. He had a real hard centre.

"What can I do for you, Mr. Mellow?"

"I've got a little job I'd like you to do for me, Mr. Faraday."

"I don't know whether you could afford my rates," I said.

He laughed. "What do you charge, Mr. Faraday?"

"I do a nice clean job for four and a half dollars inclusive, sir," I said.

He laughed again. "I like a man with a real sense of humour," he said. "Come on out to the Inn and we'll talk business."

"I'll wear my forty-dollar suit," I promised him.

"Can you make it around eight?" he said.

"Suit me fine," I said. We made with the politeness and then rang off.

"What do you make of that?" said Stella.

"Probably got an honest croupier he wants straightening out," I said. I took Stella for a bite and then drove her home.

Afterwards I went back to my house. The cops were out in front, taking the evening sun and listening to the local news on the prowl car radio. I went on upstairs and got the key. Then I found a small cardboard box, stuffed it with newspaper, stuck the key to the flap with sticky tape, wound the whole thing up with lots of brown paper.

Then I tied it good and tight with the thickest string I could find and addressed it to myself it black ink. I put the name and address on the package four times, just to make sure. Then I drove downtown again to the Central Post Office, to the window where they keep open late. The package jiggled about in the dash pocket all the way down and it kept niggling at my mind.

When I got to the post office I had it registered, using Stella's name as the sender. I paid the clerk and then put the registered package slip in a section of my billfold. That would take care it for a few hours and I could sleep nights.

Then I gunned out and hit the trail for the Jazz Inn. The Smith-Wesson felt comforting against the underside of my arm and without the key the car seemed at least half a hundred-weight lighter.

3

I drove up to the Jazz Inn and parked the car. Though it was only just gone half seven the park was already half full and through the open lobby floated the sounds all clip joints seem to have all over the world. Conversation, laughter, clinking glasses and the tinkle of a piano somewhere through the smoke—blue, lost and forlorn.

I went on up the steps and into a *patio*. There was a balcony round three sides, complemented by a bar round three walls and a foyer opening into the main gambling rooms. Upstairs there were private rooms for small parties in the higher income bracket. The main games were *chemin de fer* and roulette with baccarat and card games thrown in; the private parties were mostly for chemmy and poker.

The predominant colour scheme was walnut and green leather; Mandy had good taste, I'd say that. I nodded to the gorilla on the main door and went on in. I had some time to kill so I went up to the bar and ordered a martini. The prices were murder. I was just looking for a stool when someone tapped me on the shoulder.

Mandy Mellow was a man of about forty-five, short, chunky, broad-shouldered and with a dead white face set under jet black eyebrows that gave him a curious look. His thick black hair was brilliantly glossed but otherwise he dressed with taste. He had on a midnight blue single-breasted suit; expensive tan shoes; his impeccable grey tie was knotted in small under the points of his cream silk shirt. We shook hands.

"On the house." He nodded at the barman, who shot me a thousand dollar smile as a result.

"Have what you want, Faraday," he said. "I've got a few things to attend to, but I'll meet you up in my office sharp on eight. First door on the right at the top of the stairs."

I thanked him and went and sat down at a table. Curiously, I liked him. But I wondered what he wanted. There was a funny atmosphere in the bar. I smelt trouble. Still, it would be a fairly quiet evening by my standards. Or so I thought.

From where I was sitting I could see a long line of mirrors at the back of the bar. There was a man sitting near the end who kept staring at me in the mirror. The first thing I noticed about him was that he had on a grey suit and was wearing yellow socks. Then I saw in the mirror that he had a pink bow tie. He had grey hair too, though that didn't ring a bell. I didn't know him but he sure looked as though he knew me.

His high titter first attracted my attention. I sat on and finished my drink. A waiter came up and I ordered another. When he brought it back the guy in the grey suit came over. He staggered slightly but I was pretty sure it wasn't from drink. He looked like an albino unless his pink eyes were some sort of inflammation; I noticed something else too. He was a junky. His eyes had a brilliant glaze and there was an exaggerated cockiness in his walk that made it look like he owned the earth.

A dangerous bimbo, I thought, but a mug just the same. That was the first mistake I made about him. He sat down at my table without asking. That was his first mistake.

"I'm choosy about my company," I said. He smiled a slow smile but otherwise no reaction. He was about thirty, I should have said. His teeth were very white and even.

"You're Faraday, aren't you?" It was a statement, not a question.

I said nothing. That seemed to rile him. He leaned forward.

"You invented the miner's lamp or sump'n, didn't you?"

"That was my cousin," I told him. I was getting a bit tired of this. I stood up.

"Some other time," I said and went to walk out. He didn't like that. He stood up too, and his eyes glittered.

"We hadn't finished, sport," he said.

"I had," I told him and went to pass by.

"Don't do that," he said and put his hand on my arm. There was quite a crowd in the bar by that time so I decided to humour him. This sort of joker would be quite easy to take, but like I said, there's a time and a place.

"Let's talk outside," I said. He looked at me for a long second, his eyes dilated. He took his hand away from my arm but he kept the other in his pocket. He probably had a pig-sticker or something else in there. I began to get the idea that this wasn't a casual encounter. We went out. The barman nodded pleasantly and gave me a yard of teeth.

"Tell Mr. Mellow I'll be back in five minutes," I told him.

"Don't bank on it, joker," white hair said out of the side of his mouth. A tough baby. We went out through the *patio*. The piano died away in the distance. We walked around the rear and into the parking lot. He stopped by a large black Cadillac. I noticed it had the stencil of a hire firm on the rear door panels. That was interesting.

A young man with black hair and a swarthy face sat in the

driving seat of the Caddy. He leaned out of the open window and looked at me interestedly. He had dark glasses on; another corny gimmick.

"Let's go," said white hair. I decided this had gone far enough. I did an elegant side-step and gave white hair a nerve punch with all my strength, in his upper arm. He gave an agonized yelp. Then I put the boot in his belly. He sagged moaning against the door panel. I made sure by catching his hair and giving him three good bounces against the windshield upright. He went limp and blood came off his face on to the glass.

"Don't move, buddy," I told the driver. He sat frozen. I never take chances with junkies. I fished in white hair's pocket and came out with a small revolver with a sawn-off barrel. I put that in my pocket. Then I opened the back door of the Cadillac and shoved white hair in. He was unconscious and breathing heavily through the nose. I looked around; there was no one in the lot and the whole thing had taken perhaps ten seconds.

I leaned against the driver's door. "All right, what's the caper?" I asked him. He licked his lips and his eyes showed white. "It wasn't my idea," he said hurriedly. "I was paid just to drive you out of town."

"And then?" I asked.

"I don't know anything," he said. "Johnny was going to tell me where to drive. Honest, mister, that's straight."

I believed him. Gabriel would have, with that look on his face.

"What's your friend's name and business?" I asked.

"I only know him as Johnny," he said. "I do driving jobs for him now and again."

"Drive," I told him. "And don't mess around with amateurs. If you want to stay in this business, turn professional."

He licked his lips again and went out of the lot like a streak of black thunder. I hadn't gotten his name; not that it mattered. But I had a few things to discuss with Mandy Mellow. I went back into the Inn and took the stairs to the balcony three at a time. I went through the door without knocking. Mellow was standing by a large, glass-topped desk.

"Come in," he said ironically. His expression looked pained, but this was no time to worry about my lack of breeding.

"I'm getting a little tired of the strong-arm stuff, Mandy," I said. I must have looked tough, or perhaps I was breathing heavily. At any rate his surprise was genuine.

"I don't understand," he said. "A drink?" He indicated an expensively-loaded sideboard.

"I mean this," I said. "I didn't drive out here just to be bounced by your strong-arm boys. I can get the job done much better downtown. If I were you I'd get yourself some pro's. I've seen better stuff on Sunday night T.V."

His expression didn't change. He went over to the sideboard and started filling two long glasses from a crystal decanter.

"Really, Faraday, if it would do any good, shall I say that I don't know what you're talking about? Believe me, if I had a grudge against you, I wouldn't send amateurs."

His voice sounded patient and long-suffering. He snapped his fingers. The long velvet curtains at the two windows let into the side of the room billowed and parted. Two very big, competent-looking men stood there. They didn't need bulges around their expensive suits to tell me they were fully equipped for blasting. Mellow picked up his drinks and nodded to the two gorillas. They went on out. He handed me one of the glasses with a quizzical look.

"Convinced?" he said.

"I'm sorry," I said. "I added up two and two wrongly. I guess you know your business better at that."

"At least well enough not to leave my office door un-guarded," he said dryly.

We sat down on a long, grey upholstered divan that ran for about the length of a baseball pitch along one side of the apartment. It looked, and felt, like real leather. We drank.

"What's all this about, Faraday?" he said. I told him. He seemed to go even paler.

"Describe the driver again," he said. When I'd finished he lit a cigarette and pulled on it for a long minute.

"You won't have far to look," he said. "This is the same business I asked you over about. The driver was my younger brother."

I stared at him. "Want to spell it out?" I said.

"In brief," he said. "It was my intention to employ you to keep an eye on him."

My face must have relaxed into a grin or something; awfully bad taste. Anyway, he shot me a heavy glance.

"Can I take it that whatever we say in this room tonight will go no further?"

"I've never welshed on a client yet," I said. "I was in jail a night or two back."

He smiled. "I heard about that. My turn to say sorry."

He leaned forward. "Briefly, what I want you to do is this. My brother Paul has got himself into a situation which can only end one way. I tried to look after him. He could have had as much money as he wanted working for me, but he prefers to be independent and go his own way. With the mob he's running with, he'll finish up on a vacant lot some night."

I had a quick moment of insight—like lightning flashing in a dark room.

"Like Braganza and Ralph Johnson," I said. Mandy's mouth flew open and he sat staring at me for at least ten seconds. The silence was so intense that a mouse coughing would have sounded like a 100-megaton blast at Bikini Atoll. He caught my arm.

"Look, Faraday," he said. "All I want is out for Paul. Do it any way you like. But don't leave any trails back to me and don't let him know I hired you."

"There must be some pretty big boys at the back of this to frighten a king-wheel like you, Mandy," I said. He licked his lips, then went over to the sideboard and mixed himself another drink. I let mine stand.

"This Johnny. . . ." I said. He almost visibly winced.

"All I know is this," he said. "Paul just drives the cars for them, a sort of glorified chauffeur. No names. But one day he'll get in too deep. Then the whole town will blow up. I don't want that to happen, Faraday. Will you help me?"

"I'm already on the case," I said. "Another retainer wouldn't hurt any. But I can't guarantee results."

He went over to the desk and took out a cheque book. He wrote a cheque and handed it to me.

"Win or lose," he said. I looked at the figure. I didn't whistle but I felt like it.

"I'm not worth it," I said. I handed the slip back. "Halve it," I said. "I'm not that hard up for eating money."

"That was the retainer," he said.

I laughed. "It'll settle for the whole job."

He tore the cheque up and wrote another.

"I like you, Faraday," he said. "This town hasn't spoiled you. Pity you stick to your line. I could find a place for you in my organization."

"Then I would get spoiled," I said. "How long has he been hanging around with this crowd?"

"About a year or so," he said. "I've only ever seen him with the man called Johnny."

I finished my drink. The time seemed to tie in with the Braganza killing, give or take a month or two. That set me off on another tack.

"You realize I may dig up something about your brother that I can't cover up?" I said. "That no one can. And in that event the police may have to be called in."

"Faraday," he said with a thin smile, "I believe the military boys call it a calculated risk."

"What I want is a rundown on your brother's habits, where he hangs out and so on," I said.

He sat down at the desk and jotted down a few details on a slip of paper. "Burn this after," he said. It wasn't melodrama either. There wasn't much on the paper but I did as he said.

"Just one last thing," I said as I got up. "Have you got his address? I presume he doesn't hang out here?"

He shook his head. He named a cheap rooming house over on the other side of town. I must have looked surprised, but he didn't explain.

"People are funny," he said. I suddenly felt sorry for him. I wrote the address down in my book, then rubbed it with my thumb, to make it look like it had been there for a long time.

"Ring you in a day or two," I said and went out. I looked back at the door, but he was still standing at the desk. He didn't say good night. It was still only around nine and I had time for more social visiting. I had another free drink down at the bar and then went into a booth and called Charlie Snagge at home.

"Faraday," I said.

"Elusive Pimpernel," he said.

"I have to work now that I'm not on the force," I told him. He ignored that. "I understand you had some information that might help me," I said.

"Well," he said, in the maddeningly slow way he had. "Might help, might not. But I've been studying the case again and there's an interesting point. I got in touch with Captain Tucker and he let me have a transcript of the Johnson case in Detroit."

"All right, Holmes," I said. "I thought this was restricted information."

"It's common talk around the police canteens in this city," he said. "It was a tiny point but a link that seems to have been overlooked. But in both the Johnson and Braganza cases a young man with white hair was seen in the vicinity of the murders just a short time before."

I felt a prickling of the scalp. I took the short-barrelled revolver out of my pocket and wrapped it in my handkerchief. It must have been the blow on my head that made me so slow these days, but I didn't tell Charlie Snagge.

He was going on. "A deposition in the Braganza shooting describes a youngish man with white hair who called at a gas station in a hired car, driven by a negro chauffeur. Of course it may have no connection at all.

"If this man could be linked in some way with the Horvis shooting, there'd be a common factor . . . are you listening, Mike?"

"Sorry," I said. "I think this may be useful, Charlie. But why didn't you bring this to the notice of the official force?"

"Only just thought of it," he said. " 'Sides, blood's thicker than water. All the local forces had a go at these shootings, but they never got anywhere."

"Many thanks, Charlie," I said and hung up.

Then I rang Dan Tucker and told him about my commission from Mandy Mellow. I left the best bit to the last. When I told Dan about Johnny Whitehair I thought he was going to choke.

"And you had him right in your hands?" he said.

"Well," I said, "that was before I had the latest information. I didn't do any better than the official force, I must admit. However, it shouldn't be too difficult to trace this character through Paul Mellow. I want you to lay off for twenty-four hours and give me a chance to have a talk with him. If you want to come along it's all right with me; maybe we could go tomorrow after I meet you at H.Q."

Tucker agreed and then his voice changed. His tones were deceptively smooth.

"By the way," he said, "I shouldn't take everything Sherry Johnson tells you as gospel."

"Oh," I said.

"We had a cable back from Detroit this afternoon. They traced the photograph. Her name's not Sherry Johnson and she wasn't Johnson's sister. She was his mistress and her real name is Carol Channing. Horvis has confirmed this. Seems pretty conclusive. Thought you'd like to know."

"Thanks," I said. "Hope her cheque's good, anyway."

Then I rang off. I needed to go somewhere to sit down and think things out. My reasoning hadn't been so good since Captain Jacoby's working over, and the ends in the case kept sticking out.

7

Carol Channing

IT WAS ABOUT a quarter to ten. I got to hell out of the Jazz Inn and drove down town. There was no one around outside the gambling house and so far as I could make out no one was following me. I turned off on to the turnpike and doubled back just to make sure, but without result. The air was still blowing hot against my face, but a small breeze was beginning to spring up.

What little traffic there was went by like a dream, but on the main boulevards in town the restaurant crowd was thickening things up. On my way across I called in at the station and asked the desk sergeant for a big envelope. I put the wrapped revolver in it for Dan Tucker and the ballistics boys in the morning. I had arranged this with him on the phone. Besides, it put my suit out of line. Then I went on over to the Bissell Building.

Admiral Dewey tore me off a smart salute this time. He was learning. I went on over to the parking lot. I drove around three or four times, blipping my lights up and down, but nothing moved. There was nobody there but I was learning too. I parked the Buick as near to the Building as I could, right under the brightest light I could find. While I was doing this I was reminded of something else I should have done days ago, but for being in the tank.

I went into the phone booth and called Stella. "Just so you

won't worry," I said. "I'm sober, un-bounced, unshadowed and under cover."

"That's fine," she said. "I'm undressed and unimpressed."

I let that one go. There was an obvious answer but she'd only come back with something better. I saw there was a new phone book hanging up in front of me. It had some more dirty words on it. Looked as though Admiral Dewey was all scrambled egg and low efficiency rating.

I told Stella I'd be in around nine in the morning. There was a mirror in the booth and in it I could see part of the lobby. I had been staring at the glass for perhaps ten seconds, thinking about nothing in particular when a familiar face drifted by. It was Johnny Whitehair and he had his boy friend with him.

I flattened myself back in the booth and watched the mirror. I had to grin. Johnny had a wodge of sticking plaster across the side of his head and he looked as sore as all hell. Somehow, that reminded me of my broken tooth. The two stopped in front of the elevator. The boy opened up the door, a couple of people got out and Mellow and the trigger boy went in. They looked as though they owned the whole of L.A.

I opened the booth door and sneaked on over to the elevator. It stopped at the sixth floor. Then it started to come down. It didn't stop until it got to the lobby. I went over to the cigarette kiosk and made myself inconspicuous, but only a pair of elderly women got out. I had a pretty shrewd idea the two gorillas were on their way to see Sherry Johnson; 219 was on floor six and they didn't look as though they were on their way to a Lodge meeting.

I had two choices and not much time. I could take a chance on finding Dan Tucker at home and get him to put a tail on their car in case they gave me the slip in the building. In which case something pretty drastic might be happening up top. Or I could ask the management for a bit of co-operation and go on up myself and see what transpired. Either way it was a risk.

I thought of three bodies and Mr. X with a silenced revolver and hesitated. I could do it the police way or my way.

It didn't take me long to make up my mind. Trouble is my business and she was my client. I went on over to reception. There was a low mahogany railing with a gate in it. I went on through. There was no one at the desk behind the railing but there was another door with gold letters stencilled on it: Manager. Private.

I knocked and went on in. A woman was standing at a filing cabinet, looking at a bundle of papers. She had grey hair scraped into a bun at the back of her neck; a grey suit that matched the hair, a rat-trap mouth and square spectacles that made her look like Dr. Caligari. I took an instant indifference to her.

"This is private," she snapped.

"I can read," I said. "I want to see the manager."

"He isn't here," she said. "He's having dinner."

While this circus was going on I suddenly saw a head appear over in one corner of the room. There was another partitioned-off part of the office and I could see a desk. A little man with a bald head, pudgy face and a Charlie Chaplin mustache was sitting at the desk, eating a meal and reading a newspaper. He noticed that I had spotted him and came over.

"That will do, Miss Rutger," he said with surprising sharpness. The dragon shut the drawer of the filing cabinet with a vicious slam.

"Can I help you, sir?" he said. "No trouble I hope?"

"None," I assured him. "I'd like a little co-operation."

He hesitated; the woman still stood glaring at me.

"In private," I said pointedly. She flushed.

"You may leave us, Miss Rutger," the manager said. She went out with a sniff and shut the door none too gently. We went over towards the manager's desk.

"I have a client up in No. 219 on the sixth floor," I said. "A Miss Johnson." I showed him the copy of my P.I. licence in the celluloid folder. His eyes popped and he looked nervous.

"It's all right," I said. "There won't be any trouble—providing I get your help."

"What do you want, Mr. Faraday?" he said.

"Two characters just went up," I said. "I think there could be trouble but I want to keep an eye on the situation. Have you got a vacant room adjoining 219 where I could hole up for half an hour?"

He stared at me for a moment. "Shouldn't we get the police——" he began.

"I'm working with the police," I told him. "By the time they got here anything could happen. Do I get the co-operation?"

He nodded. "All right, Mr. Faraday, I'll get the book."

He went out and came back in a few seconds with a small black register. He had a key, too.

"No. 221 is unoccupied," he said. "I thought that would be best; it has an adjoining balcony." He gave me the key. I thanked him. Then I asked him to ring Tucker and told him what to say.

He repeated the message and then I thanked him again and went on out. I could hear him dialling the number as I closed the door. This way I could have a tail put on the pair and still be in on what was going on upstairs.

All this had taken less than a couple of minutes and I didn't figure Mellow and his friend would take any risks in the middle of a crowded building, even if they had any homicidal intentions towards the Johnson girl. I still thought of her as that. Assuming that she was in, of course . . . something else I'd forgotten to ask about. I gave a cheery smile to Little Mary Sunshine when I left the reception desk and walked on over to the elevator. Welcome to the Friendly Inn. I whined up to the sixth floor.

2

Two-two-one was a typical suite of one of the ritzier hotels. A lounge about two acres in area; lots of real leather and glass, imitation stone, a bar with a sliding door at one end; too many ashtrays; a master bedroom, two dressing rooms and a bathroom. I stood in the room in the red dusk of the neon signs and smelt danger the way kids can hear a sweet wrapper crackling a mile off.

I went on through the master bedroom; the walls seemed to be made of mink and it made Buckingham Palace look like a two-bit flop joint. Sherry Johnson appeared to be home; I looked through the master bedroom window. A pale lozenge of light from her windows was stencilled on the tiling of the balcony next door. I went through the window and over the low balcony separating the two suites with all the grace and agility of a musk-ox.

I prowled along the balcony; it was a big one, floored with ceramic tiles and had a lot of potted plants, frosted glass sun-screens, Italian cane chairs, ornamental tile-top tables; that sort of thing. There were big beach umbrellas in metal holders anchored to the floor at intervals. The balcony was bigger than the one in 221 and occupied a corner site. I looked over the edge of the roof.

There was a fire escape that went down a short way below, with a wicket gate on to the balcony; it was unlocked. Convenient. I saw that directly below was the parking lot but I couldn't see any particular car very well from that height; I turned back to the windows and eased forward carefully. I was facing into the big main room where I'd sat and talked with Sherry Johnson. I couldn't see anything at first. Two of the big shaded lamps were on and one of the wall lights, but the interior still looked dim. Then I saw shadows and a man walked across a gap in the drapes, which were half pulled across the window. It was Paul Mellow. Looked like I had won the kewpie doll.

I stayed put for a minute or two but couldn't hear anything. I got a little closer and then more figures crossed the interior. They seemed to be moving into the next room for a light suddenly went on in there. There were no drapes across this one. I gum-shoed my way farther down the terrace and found another wrought iron balcony railing across my path. It was only waist high and I almost stepped over. I was on another balcony with the same sort of tiled floor. There was a clipped box hedge, let into wooden trunking, more tables and beach umbrellas.

I got near the window and stopped. Sherry Johnson was standing inside; the room was a bedroom and she wore some sort of yellow house-coat. The man with white hair was doing most of the talking and Paul Mellow was standing by, looking dramatic. I got as near as I dared but the sound-track was still out. It was a bit comic. I could stay here, hear nothing and understand nothing and perhaps follow when the two gorillas left. Or I could barge in and play it by ear from then on.

As it turned out, the problem was solved for me. I had been out there perhaps ten minutes, making a very good target from the street against the lit windows. When I next looked up the tableau was in action. Paul Mellow had got Sherry Johnson by the lapels and her housecoat was gaping open; the girl was lunging at the junky with her hand raised to strike and he had opened a pig-sticker and was waving it in front of her face.

I thought it was time to intervene. I set off at a smart trot towards the window, six feet away. I made a grand job of it. What I hadn't seen was that the nearest metal table had wide splayed legs coming out from the centre like a rosette; I found one of them with my foot. I went down with a helluva crash, the table went the other way with a noise like all the symphony orchestras in Christendom were tuning up and to make matters worse the table rolled and hit the window with one big bang as a finale.

The group inside froze for one split second, then the girl went down and the two figures vanished from view. I got up cursing and put my shoulder at the big windows. Unlike the movies they didn't give and I had only a bruised shoulder for my trouble. Then I saw Sherry Johnson get up unhurt so I didn't worry. I went over the balcony like Jesse Owens in a hurry and then some mug in a prowl car set his siren going as the police wagon I had sent for, to shadow Johnny Whitehair, turned into Corona Avenue.

That left me two choices. To leg it down the fire escape and be in at the kill in the parking lot. Or to hustle out through 221 and hope the lift jammed. As it happened I chose the latter but the way the police were organized that night I don't suppose it would have mattered. I got out through 221 without wrecking any furniture and found the lift was already way down.

I hit the exit stairs but I needn't have bothered. When I made the sidewalk with smoking brogues there was an interested crowd in front of the building, a couple of sheepish coppers in a prowl car and one useless hire car stashed in the parking lot.

These boys were good, I had to give them that. The couple were probably riding a street car a couple of blocks away, half-way through the baseball results by now. I left it to Tucker to blast the prowl men and went back in to thank the manager. While I was in the lobby there was a call for me. Mary Sunshine risked her dentures in handing the phone to me. She was probably impressed by my footwork. Come to think of it I had been pretty good on the stairs tonight.

It was Dan Tucker. I told him what had happened and held the phone out at arm's length. Then I told him good night. As I went to ring off I could hear him telling someone in the station to get the prowl car wavelength on the R/T.

I got back in the lift and rode up. I went in through 221 again and out on to the balcony. I straightened up the mess I had made with the tables. I heard a car gun in the lot below. I looked down and saw the prowl car going away. It seemed to sneak down the avenue. They didn't use the siren this time. I sighed and went on over and tapped at Sherry Johnson's window. This would be great work if you had a clue what it was all about.

3

There was a pause and then the curtains slid back. Sherry Johnson looked white and startled. Then she relaxed and slid the bolts. I went on in.

"It's easier when the window's unlocked," I said. She said nothing but took me through the bedroom into the lounge. I sat down in a leather chair and feathered smoke at the ceiling. She went over to the sideboard and made a great noise of clinking bottles. She came back over and handed me another long drink. She looked better already.

We tapped glasses and drank. She fumbled in her pocket and produced a crumpled package of cigarettes. It was empty. I gave her one of mine and lit it.

"Thanks," she said, but she wasn't referring to the light. She went and sat down on the divan, smoked for a minute or two and swung her legs. She seemed to have on silver lamé pyjamas. Usually I think that sort of thing corny, but they looked good on her.

"Friends of yours?" I asked. Her eyes widened and she stiffened.

"I should say not," she said. "Does this look like friendship?" She pulled away her housecoat and bared a shoulder. Angry red marks were already turning to deep bruises. She had a point there.

"I just wondered," I said. You haven't seen them before?"

She shook her head. "They told me to stop asking too many questions," she said. "One of them, the nasty one, had sticking plaster on his face."

"I know—that was me," I said. She smiled again then; it lit up the dim room briefly and some of the fear went from her face.

"They said they knew I'd engaged a detective and warned me to leave town. They said they'd taken care of you."

"Slightly exaggerated," I said. She got up and went to refill my glass.

"What was the pantomime in the bedroom?" I asked.

"That was the horrible part," she said. She shuddered.

"They pushed me inside and the fair one told me to strip. The other man—Mellow was it?—was frightened and kept saying they should leave. The other one shouted him down and told me to get my clothes off and get on the bed. He was going to work me over with the knife, to teach me a lesson, he said."

She stopped momentarily and I waited for her to go on. It

was pleasant and quiet in the dusk; the heat of the day had gone at last and the noises from the boulevard were muted and far away.

"And?" I prompted her.

"The young one got hold of me. I told them to get out and started to strike at them. Then you fell down outside the window and they ran off."

We looked at one another for a long moment and then she burst out laughing. I joined in, though what the hell for, I didn't know. She gave me my drink and sat down in a chair, still shaking. I knew the laughter would turn to hysterics if I didn't do something so I caught hold of her by the shoulders and pulled her against me.

"It's all right," I said. "It's all right, it's all over now."

She came up against me; her hair was fragrant against my face and her skin smelt of violets or whatever it is women use in bathrooms. Anyway, I'm as human as most guys, or so they tell me, and this was definitely a twelve-cylinder job. She put up her mouth to be kissed and I felt her lips, full and tender in the semi-darkness.

We kissed. It was a long one and when I came down to earth again I found I'd spilled my drink all over the carpet. I always go into these things ill-prepared. Not that it mattered. No one was complaining. I blotted out a mental picture of Stella and went in for some more. We were at an interesting stage in the proceedings when the door bell buzzed softly in the silence.

I suppressed a natural oath and Sherry bounced out of the settee, doing up the buttons of her pyjama top. She was grinning and found time to stick out her tongue at me as she waltzed towards the bedroom. This was too good an evening to waste, so I de-frosted my face with an effort, straightened my tie and opened the door. It was the manager. He was all apologetic and deferential.

"Is everything all right, Mr. Faraday?" he asked. "I wondered about Miss Johnson. A dreadful thing to happen in the hotel. . . ."

D

"Come on in," I told him as he babbled on. "She won't sue you, if that's what you're talking about."

He looked pained. "I just came up to tell Miss Johnson that under the circumstances we propose to make no charge for the accommodation. Unless she would like to move to another suite. . . ."

"That's up to her," I said. "She's been rather upset. If I were you I'd just tap on the other door and explain."

"A good idea, Mr. Faraday." He looked relieved. I thought this would be a proper time for me to organize myself for ten minutes. I pencilled a note on my scratch pad, folded it and left it under my drink. I had just got the main door half-closed when I heard the two of them talking as she came out of the bedroom. Besides, it would look better to the manager if I disappeared for a bit. I rode down to the ground floor, nodded to the doorman, who was new to me; apparently Admiral Dewey had gone off duty. Little Mary Sunshine had stolen away too, which was a relief.

I lit a cigarette and enjoyed the night air. Then I went over to the Buick parked under the lamp and made a big thing about driving away. I gunned the engine, gave plenty of tyre snatch on the tarmac and with headlights blazing, drove ostentatiously up the far end of the parkway, about a quarter of a mile; made quite a business of turning on to the boulevard, then cut my lights and sneaked in again behind a board fence on a building lot. I parked the car, set the brake, put up the hood, took a final look round and then locked the car.

Then I footed it back along the parking lot and up the fire escape in front of the main suites. Nothing moved anywhere but I stayed still for perhaps five minutes until I had satisfied myself. When I got to the place just below the balcony I found there was one of those fancy escapes, which extend only from the top; this was the most difficult part of the evening and threatened to interfere seriously with my pleasure.

Rather than risk a *pas de deux* with a trash can I was about to swallow my pride and go in around the main entrance, when I remembered my belt; I took it off and by jumping as high as I could and holding the loop up over my head I managed to catch a metal bar on the bottom of the ladder at the fourth or fifth attempt. It came down without a squeak and I was on the balcony within seconds. Dead easy, I said smugly, but I happened to look at my watch and found it was past one; I had been away half an hour already. Dead easy, my foot.

I tip-toed over to the main window of Sherry's suite and was surprised to see the manager still there. He was standing finishing a drink and making extravagant gestures with his hands, like he was trying to smooth things down. I thought he was going to kiss her hand when he left about five minutes later. I sat at one of the tables briefly before going in and looked at the sky. The stars looked big and remote; they seemed painted on and somehow the lights of the city looked almost beautiful by contrast. Walden Pond wasn't in my line at all.

When I figured the manager had been gone too long to come back I went over to the bedroom window. It was still unlocked and I slipped through and locked it behind me. Then I went on into the lounge. I don't know what I expected, but Sherry was sitting in a big chair, smoking a cigarette and looking about fourteen years old. She had on the same house coat and her legs were bare; on her feet were a tiny pair of black Oriental-style slippers. She looked good enough to eat and I felt hungry.

"You took your time," she said. She looked very calm and grave, as though she had men all figured out years ago.

"I thought I'd give the manager a chance," I said. "He only gets old ladies and teenagers to deal with usually."

She laughed, showing those perfect teeth. She patted the arm of the chair next to her.

"Come and sit here," she said. "But get me a drink first."

I went over and fixed a long one, more for my benefit than hers. My hand wasn't quite steady when I brought the drinks back; for the second time that evening I spilled my glass. Must be getting old, I told myself. The mid-thirties are a bad time for P.I.s. You feel more like it than you ever did, but you get

less opportunities and when they do come you wonder if you'll
be up to it physically.

I needn't have worried that night. All the signs were pro-
pitious and Venus was definitely in conjunction with Taurus,
or something about that price-range. We didn't talk much;
we just sat and finished our drinks and then we kissed. After
what seemed about five hours and when it was around 2 a.m.
as far as I could make out through the roaring in my ears. I
started to undo the buttons of her house coat. She didn't stir
but seemed to lean forward to make it easier.

She was nude underneath, as I knew she would be. I cupped
a breast; it was firm as a young grapefruit and much about
the same size. I couldn't get enough of this but before I could
proceed any further she undid the remaining buttons for me
and spreadeagled her legs with a moan. The coat fell to the
ground and she was nude except for the slippers. We fell into
the chair in a deep kiss.

"Put out the lights, Mike, and take me to bed," she panted.

Hell, what could I do? She had a magnificent figure and
her knees were hard and firm as small apples under my hands.
She was a regular fruit store. I had difficulty in carrying her;
she was a tall girl and heavy too, but her legs were really
beautiful. She had flesh where it mattered but she was fine
and trim in all the right places as well. I was breathing pretty
heavily when I got to the bed and I fell on it; before we hit
the bedspread, she was already unbuttoning my slacks and
helping herself.

"No holds barred," she breathed softly in my ear, fascin-
ated and absorbed in what she was doing. We were at it until
around five as near as I could judge. She made love in a dry,
athletic style which had great fierceness and passion; but she
liked to hold off and get the most out of it. She was surprisingly strong and what she didn't know about sex would have
filled half a line in the city phone book—in their smallest type.

When she got the most out of something she tried a varia-
tion; she knew what she liked and she made you like it. If
there was anything she didn't want or didn't like, I couldn't

supply it, that was for sure. And yet, surprisingly, there was nothing offensive about her leading; if there could be such a thing, she enjoyed sex like a woman and practised it like a lady.

When we had pretty near worn ourselves and our ingenuity out with it, we fell asleep. I woke up around half past five. We were both lying on top of the bed, stark-naked, and I interested myself in making another inventory. Then I saw her eyelids quiver and I knew she was watching me; it was still dark and the room was in semi-shadow but the neons spilled a little light through the blinds.

"All right?" I asked.

"Yes," she said, opening her eyes. "You're pretty good," she said candidly.

"You're not bad yourself," I said. "Nine out of ten, I'd say."

"Oh," she said coolly. "Where did I miss out?"

"Well, I'm sorry we didn't get around to the ninety-seventh," I said.

She crinkled her face. "The ninety-seventh?"

"Aren't the Hindus supposed to have ninety-seven basic positions for making love?" I said.

"Oh, that. . . ." She threw back her head and laughed. "Not very enterprising, are they?"

"We'd better save something for another time," I said, chancing my arm. She opened her eyes wide, as though the idea had never occurred to her.

"Perhaps," she said.

"I'll take a rain-check on that," I said.

She clasped her hands behind her head. I fished in my pocket; part of my suit was lying on the floor somewhere in the bedroom and I had to crawl around in the dark, which amused her no end. I eventually found some cigarettes, lit two and gave her one. She spread out her legs and we lay back, side by side, looked at the ceiling and smoked. It was going to be a hot day again. The room was still warm and there was just that little touch of coolness before the dawn when you can always tell it's going to be a scorcher.

"Did you know Ralph Johnson long?" I asked.

There was such a heavy silence that I thought she had gone to sleep. Except that I felt her thighs stiffen on the bedclothes.

"How did you know?" she asked at last, in a small voice.

"That Ralph Johnson wasn't your brother?" I said. "Only a little while. The L.A. police got a run-down on you. They told me your real name is Carol Channing and that Johnson was your boy friend."

She turned to face me; surprisingly, I saw only candour in her eyes.

"So you don't want to go on with the case?" she said.

"I didn't say that," I said. "But the story—the assembly line-up—was a lot of old wind and blarney, wasn't it?"

She nodded and puffed at her cigarette. "Does it matter?"

"Not really," I said. "You're paying the expenses. Was there any truth at all in what you told me?"

"Some," she said defensively. "Basically, what I wanted you to know was the truth. Ralph was my lover, not my brother. But I find it doesn't always pay to put all your cards on the table. Most people aren't too keen to help a girl whose lover has been found shot, but they're more sympathetic to brothers and sisters."

"You've got a point there," I said. "Right, take that as read. But why all the mystery? Why not level with me?"

"I have—where it counts," she said fiercely. "Ralph was murdered, by whom I don't know; what for doesn't concern you. I pay you to dig out the truth, to find out something about his killers."

"And not to make love to you," I said. "Okay, I'm in my place. I'm sorry. Let me know when you get any more client-employee relationships coming up and I'll put my pyjamas on."

She leaned over and kissed me. It was long and lingering and the fronts of our bodies were touching all down their length.

"I'm sorry, too," she breathed. "I didn't mean to let off steam. We're friends, aren't we?"

"Looks like it," I said with a grin, glancing at our reflections in the mirror. "But nobody in this case has yet levelled with me about anything, except the official detective in charge; the simple, city flatfoot who gets paid for getting his ass shot off. The honest citizens have been so busy corkscrewing the truth, that nobody's yet been able to get at it."

"Would it matter?" she said. "I've simply engaged you to do a job for me. The less you know, the better so far as I'm concerned. I'm not asking you to do anything illegal to help me, if that's what you mean."

She had me there. "And your two boy-friends? You didn't know them before?" I asked.

"I told you last night," she said and there was a ring in her voice which was absolutely convincing. I sighed and shifted towards her.

"All right," I said. "I'll play ball."

"Good boy," she said. We kissed again.

4

The curtains stirred in the breeze. A little light was just starting to come into the room, etching the furniture in shadow. The neons had gone out about half an hour before, except for one day-and-night sign opposite, all pink and green, which gave a surrealist tinge to the dusk in the bedroom. Carol shivered and stubbed out her second cigarette in a black onyx tray. She got up, put on a pair of high-heeled shoes and walked around the end of the bed. She looked pretty good, especially with the high heels, and I swivelled to follow her.

"I hate this time of day," she said. There was an emptiness in her voice.

"I usually sleep through it," I told her. She walked over near the window. There was a woman's big dressing-table there, all crystal and silver fittings. On top was a rectangular mirror, split into many segments. The bottom part was in darkness but I could see Carol's head and breasts, etched in green and pink from the sign, reflected back at a dozen different angles.

"I sometimes wonder where everything ends up," she said.

"It helps to think serious thoughts, even when you're twenty-four," I told her.

She shivered again. "I didn't mean that," she said.

"Life is like this mirror, I sometimes think. I've got a big one in my bedroom at home. Every day it reflects a little bit more of my life; the bad things, the good things, and I can see it all in my face when I sit in front of it, making up to go out in the evening.

"In the morning, in summer, the mirror reflects back the sunlight and everything seems lovely, you know, like when you're seventeen. That's the beginning of life. Then at mid-day the shadows have grown longer and you look at your face in the mirror; you see that the light is harder and there are lines you didn't think you had. Then, in the evening, the shadows get blacker and longer and quite suddenly, before you know it, the light has all gone, the darkness is here and everything's finished. Nothing but darkness and death."

She paused. I joined her at the window. The night wind rustled the blind. "You get a lot of value out of your mirrors," I said lightly. "The one in my room never does that. It just reflects back the same cock-eyed guy from day to day."

She smiled but still stood looking into the glass. From where I was standing I couldn't see much; just darkness, sliced by the green and red segments of the neon. The way she put it, it did sound kinda spooky. A queer kid, but nice. She thought too much.

"A lot of people in this world never get to be twenty-four," I said. "Sling out your mirror and live a long and happy life."

She did give a laugh at that. She came into my arms all of a sudden.

"Oh, Mike," she said. "I've never met anyone quite so matter-of-fact as you. It's reassuring in some ways. I'm glad we met."

"Even though it's costing you expenses-plus a day," I said.

She thumped me then. It hurt and I pinched her. After we finished horsing around we went in the shower. She drew the blinds and put on the light. We stood under the scalding water and soaped one another. It was like the dawn of the world. It was too good to last and we both knew it. Then she went out to dress and I stayed to finish towelling myself. When I came out she was half standing, one knee on a chair. She had on the smallest black suspender belt I had ever seen, the black shoes and the sheerest nylons, which she was adjusting. I took one look and knew what I wanted. I went at her in a run leaving the towel way behind.

"Mike!" she shouted, but it was delight and not approbation in her voice. I gave it to her the best way I knew how. We went at it hot and strong; her legs were somewhere around my neck but I didn't give a damn. We both seemed to think it was pretty urgent. I know it was the best quarter of an hour of my life up to now. When we finished we both took a long time to come apart.

"You must think I'm a loose woman," she said.

"I thought you were pretty tight," I said. She aimed a blow at me.

"Bastard!" she said, but the way she bit my ear wasn't serious. Then I dressed her, then I dressed myself. When I came back from the bedroom I could smell food. I went into the lounge and found a fully laden trolley, with enough stuff on it to last a couple of weeks. The waiter had gone.

She had chosen a white dress with a floral pattern and she had done something to her hair while I had been away, which made it look stunning. We had breakfast sitting there with the sun blazing away up over the foothills, and the morning wind rustling the curtains and I thought the life of a P.I. might be worth it, after all. It was the high peak of the case and I knew I should never hit this stride again. I kissed her on the cheek when I got up to go.

"Thanks for everything," I said, and meant it. She clung to me for a moment and then slowly pushed me away. "Call me, Mike," she said. I nodded and went on out. I walked down to the lift like I had blocks of foam rubber under my size nines.

8

Paul Mellow

I GOT OUT at the ground floor, walked across the lobby and out through the main entrance. It was only around half-seven and no one appeared to be on duty. The air smelled good. I went on over to the parking lot. The car was drenched with a heavy dew and it took three pulls to start her. I tooled gently back along the parkway and stopped the car near the board fence where I had the shoot-out with my friend. I must have slipped a cog not to have thought of it sooner.

I put the car in front of the fence to shield what I was doing, though there was no one about. After a few minutes I found a biggish hole near the top, which had new edges. If the bullet had gone on through without hitting anything else it would be useless to look any farther, for it was a vacant lot beyond and it could have carried a long way. I went back down the fence. There was a small gate let into it. It was unlocked and I went on in. When I got back to the hole I found I was in luck for once.

The bullet had deflected off a metal stanchion belonging to a telephone pole and there, ten minutes later, I found it embedded in the thick timber. It took me another five to prise it out with a pen-knife. It had spread out, of course, but it should be an easy job for the ballistics boys. At least it would tie up, or not, with the joker who was leaving his calling card.

But there couldn't be two choppers operating with silenced revolvers of the same calibre in the same area.

I put the shapeless piece of lead in my pocket and drove off across town. I couldn't find a place to park the Buick near my office so I took it in for a wash and polish and then rode up in the creaking lift. As usual, Bert Dexter was nowhere about; it was still a little before nine but even so Stella had already completed two letters and the coffee was beginning to come to the boil. She was sitting behind my desk, pert, freshly groomed and as clean-scrubbed as the morning.

She grinned as I came in through the door and for a minute or two I felt a heel. Then it passed; we had no formal arrangement and I had to let off steam sometimes. I dictated a few notes over a cup of coffee. She never said a word about anything, but she looked quietly sure of herself, like she had caught me out in something crooked. Very likely she had.

Besides being very efficient, Stella was very beautiful, I thought to myself; but not in an obvious, sexy way. More than once I caught myself glancing at her stockings. These were legs I had never seen above the knee. Curious thing was that the sight of them aroused more interest in me than the sight of Carol Channing naked. Strange. There was a Thought for the Week, if you like.

While I sipped another cup of coffee I gave Stella a run-down on some of the more outstanding events of the last twenty-four hours. She frowned and bit on her pencil.

"Not a very impressive effort," she said of my débâcle outside the Channing girl's window. I let that go, too. The door opened and Bert Dexter came in. He nodded in a friendly manner and sat down at his desk. The room was so big it was like being at opposite ends of a baseball court. When we wanted to talk it was really easier to use the phone. I suppose it would have been better to have partitioned the room off, but we never got around to it.

I asked Stella to call Mandy Mellow and tell him I was making progress and then sauntered over to Bert's desk. He was quite the nicest guy I knew; almost without exception among the people I had met he was completely without a personal axe to grind, which was a rarity in this world. We ran off at the mouth about this and that while Stella made her calls. Around ten I shut up shop for an hour and rode Stella down to the ground floor. I had a little job for her to do. We walked around the next block to collect the car.

We drove out of the garage and across town. It was another beautiful day or would have been if they could have found some way of extracting the smog from the atmosphere, the cars from the through-ways and the noise from the ear-drums. Otherwise, like I said, it was real swell. When we got to the house one of the two cops on duty came out on to the porch. It was the tough-looking, pleasant one who had been on before.

" 'Morning, Mr. Faraday. 'Morning, miss." He looked pleased with himself. He'd probably been at the coffee beans again.

"This came special delivery this morning." He pointed over at my desk. It was the registered package containing the key. This was getting to be a damned nuisance. Ever since Margaret Standish had given it me, it had burned a hole in my pocket; I daren't hang on to it, and yet I never could find time to go down to the bank and use it. I had an idea that the whole of the case was somehow wrapped up in it, but I didn't want to move until the heat was off. That was why I wanted Stella to come up.

When the patrolman went out into the kitchen again I tore the package open; shredded it until the address and postal details were illegible and then put the key in Stella's handbag. It fitted nicely on her key-ring with a lot of other stuff.

"Hang on to this," I told her. "It might make the difference between eating and really living."

Then I drove her downtown again; and decanted her outside the office. It was a quarter to eleven so I drove on over to Central Police H.Q. The Goon Squad was just coming off as I arrived and apes in policemen's caps were spreading out in all directions along the sidewalks. It made me feel nervous. I reported to the desk sergeant and then went on up to Dan Tucker's office.

It had the same sort of lino, carpets, institutional furniture as Jacoby's precinct office, except that Tucker's was clean; surprising what you can do with soap, water and wax. Dan Tucker sat solidly behind his desk; there were two of the inevitable apple cores in the ashtray before him. He looked clean, well shaved and rested.

He nodded with gloomy pleasure when I came in, motioned me into a steel and leather arm-chair. He dumped wads of official paper in brown bindings, and card folders into my hands. Then he grunted again, picked up the phone and leaned back. "Excuse me if I get on with some work while you read," he said. "We do have other cases on the county files."

I looked at the folders. There was an autopsy report on the late Horvis; another on Braganza—I noticed that the sour MacNamara had carried out this one as well. He seemed to have the monopoly. The minutes ticked by as I read on. There were reports on the hire firm and the car used for the getaway after the Horvis shooting; whoever had done the job had worn gloves. The bullets in the two shootings matched, as Tucker had told me; then there was a file from Detroit on the Ralph Johnson murder.

This interested me more. I noticed that very little was said about Carol Channing. There was a reference to a man with white hair—Dan Tucker had appended a couple of pencilled notes—on two occasions; both limited to about five lines. One the gas station woman in the Braganza case, the other a witness in the Johnson shooting. I read for perhaps half an hour and then threw the heavy bundle back on the desk. There was very little new that we didn't already know. We were really no further forward and yet I felt we were very close to the big break.

"How you make out with Miss Channing?" said Tucker suddenly.

"I've been in close contact with her," I told him. His face was inscrutable but there was a twinkle at the back of his eyes; I wondered for a minute whether he'd had a couple of his goons staked out round the Bissell Building last night. What the hell, anyway, I thought; it's a free country.

"About that revolver. . . ." I said. Tucker's face lit up.

"You've done well, Mike," he said. "This is what we've been waiting for. I've been on to the D.A."

"I thought you said last night——" I went on.

"That was last night," he said hurriedly. "Neither of us did too well last night."

"You can say that again," I said.

"The revolver . . . well it hadn't been fired, and I don't think it has anything to do with the shootings, but it had one or two prints. They were a bit blurred but one was useable. It's on file."

He rubbed his hands with suppressed excitement. He went over to the window blinds and pulled the slats of the Venetian shutters closed. The room went into darkness.

"Take a look at this." He sat down at the desk and pressed a button. I hadn't noticed but there was a small slide projector at one end of his table. A fan whirred and a beam of light picked out a rectangle on a small roll-down screen at the other side of the room. Dan Tucker swore. "Damn this thing," he said. Sounded as though he had burned himself. He fumbled around in the gloom and then a picture slid on to the screen.

It seemed to be a group of cons. There was a negro and two other men standing against a wall in those rough grey costumes that make them look like something out of an old James Cagney movie, only one of the men interested me but his face was too screwed up to make out properly. Another picture went on; this was a good, clear head and shoulders, taken full face. I didn't need to look any further. Despite the bruise on the temple, the open-neck shirt and the flat, grainy photography I would have known him anywhere.

"That's him," I said. "Only now he's got a bruise to match on the other side."

Tucker's breath went out in a long whoosh. He switched the machine off. Then sunlight came back into the room. He came over from the blind.

"Gone With The Wind was better acted," I said. Tucker flicked me a piece of pasteboard. He got on the phone. "And don't forget the airports," I heard him say.

I stared at the index card. It contained another paste-on photograph; it was divided into three sections, two profiles and a full-face. The typed data said; Sirocco, Johnny, alias John Meacham, alias James Mitchum. He was a small-time hood-lum who had done two longish stretches in the state peniten-tiary, one for murder, another for robbery with violence. There was a lot more too about dope peddling, being in possession of narcotics, sexual assaults against women and a bit of procure-ment on the side. A thoroughly likeable character.

"Shouldn't be too difficult now," I said. "But this still doesn't tie Sirocco in with the silenced revolver. From what I can see, he used an entirely different type of gun. In fact there's no evidence about anything except that he wouldn't qualify for the scout movement. The gun I took off him hadn't even been fired."

Dan scratched his chin. His chair creaked under him as he sat back and folded his hands.

"True," he said. "But once we nab him, things will start beginning to crack. In the first place you wouldn't expect him to carry a gun with that record unless he was actually on a job. Secondly, he may lead us to the chief joker."

I conceded a couple of good points. Whatever else we might have discussed would have to wait, as there came a sudden buzz on the intercom.; Tucker spoke into it and then turned to me.

"Horvis just arrived," he said. "You'd better let me start off. I'll introduce you and afterwards you can take it on. Though I don't think you can squeeze out any angles that we haven't thought of. He sighed. "It's been a heavy case."

2

Horvis had come and gone. We hadn't learned anything new but it was pretty obvious he was on the up and up. Dan

Tucker leaned back in his chair, took an apple out of the drawer and started to scrunch. I put up with this for a bit and then went out. I wanted to find a toilet. The desk sergeant directed me. I washed my hands and went on out. Seemed to me the police dossiers had produced little except for tying Sirocco in with the killings.

I knocked on Tucker's door and went in. It was quite a surprise. The other chair was occupied by Captain Jacoby.

"Come in," said Tucker without looking up. Jacoby's neck turned a dull red.

"I didn't know you were planning out the police concert or I would have waited outside," I said.

Tucker grinned and indicated a chair. Jacoby scowled. He looked like Akim Tamiroff without the talent. He wore maroon socks under brown trousers and the hairy suit made him look simian; he reminded me of an ape I once saw at the Bronx Zoo. This one had a sore ass; I couldn't tell about Jacoby. He was sitting down and he didn't wriggle his can so I guessed I shouldn't take the analogy too far.

"The captain's come to give me some advice," Tucker explained.

"They run out of ideas down at the precinct?" I asked.

Jacoby's flush flushed. He cleared his throat. "Now look, Faraday," he started to rumble. Tucker cut in. He seemed overlong on tact today.

"Let's relax gentlemen, shall we?"

Before he could get on to anything else, I thought I'd produce my little bonus. I picked the lead ingot out of my pocket and plopped it down on to Tucker's blotter.

"Compliments of the management," I said. The two men goggled.

"What's this?" said Tucker. I told him.

"If my hunch is correct the bullet will match up with the others," I said. "It wouldn't take Einstein to link up this little lot. Whoever is doing the skin-perforating around here, has left a complete set by now."

No one said anything for a minute. Jacoby's ugly face looked like an Indian totem pole. Then a choking noise came out of Dan Tucker's face.

"And you mean to tell me that this happened some nights ago?" he started.

"Take the strain off your gall bladder," I told him. "It wouldn't have done any good. There was no point in mentioning it and I was in enough trouble already."

Tucker looked down disgustedly at the shapeless chunk of lead.

"Well, all right," he said at length. "But next time, if a fly leaves a hoof mark on your wristlet watch, tell me . . . that's what I'm paid for and I want to know. It may be important."

I tried to look frightened—for the record. Then Tucker buzzed for one of his flunkeys and we all went up to a lab on the second floor of the building. A small, wizened chemist in a white coat took the bullet. He labelled it, took it away and fussed about with microscopes and things. About a year and a half later he came back.

"They match," he said in an expressionless voice. "Send you prints and a record card down."

"Thanks, Mac," Tucker said. All his staff seemed to be expatriate Scotsmen. He rubbed his hands. We went down to his office again. Jacoby excused himself. He seemed excited about something. He shot me a venomous glance, shook hands absently-mindedly with Tucker and went away pretty quickly. I sat down and drank a cup of coffee. After, I checked out with Stella on the phone and told her I'd pick her up for lunch. Then it was pretty close on midday. Time we were moving.

3

We got in the same black prowl car and drove across town. It was time we had a word with Paul Mellow. Tucker didn't use the siren. The address Mandy had given me was over in a cheap neighbourhood. It was a surprisingly long way and Tucker was sweating as the sun beat through the windshield as he drove.

I took off my coat but it didn't do much good. A brilliant blue sky emphasized the essential ugliness of much of L.A. We passed a section of cheap delicatassens, T.V. hire stores with fluorescent signs losing in competition with the sun; a row of hackies outside a bus terminal; super-markets, liquor stores, tailors' shops, two or three B-feature cinemas, a drive-in hash joint; a couple of Italian restaurants.

There was a rash of gaudy signs; Funeral Parlor, Eat at Joe's, Hi-Lite Laundry. Civilization spitting out the last remnants of respectability. It wasn't Skid Row but it was trying. Tucker stopped the car in a dirt yard outside a freight depot. A hooter sounded mournfully across the sunlit acres and there came the clitter-clatter of freight cars being shunted. A couple of negroes in brilliant red shirts went by at the end of an alley.

There was a whole mess of frame buildings; old women were sitting on the stoops of sagging porches. Paint was peeling from everything and the air smelled of stale cabbage and yesterday's gravy.

"You sure this is the right place?" asked Tucker reflectively.

"Perhaps he likes to be private," I said.

"You can say that again," he said gloomily. "He ain't likely to be disturbed here."

He flicked an apple core over a board fence in disgust. It bounced on a pile of trash cans and a crowd of flies rose buzzing in the close air. The house we wanted, 7438 Folsom, was a big rambling frame building set back on a weed-grown pavement and sandwiched in between two crumbling brownstone apartment blocks. I had seen such places in Dodge and some of the old Western cowtowns where you expect such picturesque survivals, but I hadn't known they still existed in L.A. Still, I had been learning a lot of things in the past week.

We picked our way through screaming children, along a boardwalk and up some old wooden steps. 7438 had a big entrance hall, dark and dirty; the doors were painted in varying shades of chocolate brown, all of it peeling. A big negro passed us in the gloom as we went in through the wedged-open door. A frosted glass lobby had once contained clean windows. There was another door with a card pinned to it. It said : JANITOR. Tucker knocked. It sounded like drum-fire in the hall and I hoped no one upstairs had heard it.

There was a shuffling noise and an enormous woman peered out from behind the door suspiciously. As far as I could make out she was the same size all the way down. She had iron-grey hair, a face like Joe Stalin and a cigarette burned in a corner of her mouth. She kept the door on the chain.

"Yeah," she said. Her voice sounded like a cold chisel going through metal tubing. She didn't take the cigarette out of her mouth. It was probably fixed, anyway.

"Apartment 22?" I asked. She jerked her thumb towards the ceiling. "Sixth floor back," she said. She slammed the door and we heard her feet going away. She didn't believe in shooting her mouth off.

"Nice old lady," I said.

"You asking me or telling me?" said Tucker. We went on up. The smells seemed to get worse the higher we went. On the first floor there was more chocolate brown paint, doors with children crying behind them, an uncarpeted hallway. Dim bulbs burned on every landing; they only seemed to make the place darker. Footsteps echoed hollow on the bare boards, once or twice dim figures passed us in the gloom.

I felt the sweet bulge of my holster under my arm-pit. We seemed to have been walking for about three hours and I could hear Tucker breathing heavily in this airless vault. We stopped for a moment about four flights up. A radio was blaring through paper-thin walls; I leaned against the door for a second and a fat cockroach scuttered away from my hand.

"No one in his senses would live here for choice," whispered Tucker, his head against my ear. Pretty much my impression. Could be an accommodation address. There were a number of fascinating suppositions.

A board creaked as Dan Tucker moved his agile bulk and I followed him up the next flight of stairs. When we got to the sixth floor, I could see that the stairs still led upwards into the darkness. Down below, the stairwell was fretted by the bright sunlight which came through the open door of the hall; above us, sun spilled through a dusty skylight about a hundred feet higher up. In between the two extremes there was only shadow and the shapes of the stair railings printed in little stipples of light.

I saw Tucker had got his gun out so I eased mine out of the shoulder holster; I had a short-barrel fitting and it had the silencer already on. Tucker was still in front and I couldn't get past him without making a heck of a noise. We went down the end of the corridor. Nothing stirred. There was a piece of paper pinned alongside the last door. It had a number typed on it; 22.

Tucker knocked. The raps went echoing down the stairwell. There was the faintest scuttering behind the door, then silence. I could feel the sweat trickling down me. I looked at Tucker and he looked at me. He tried the door-handle. I noticed he stood well away from the edge of the door, in the shelter of the wall. The door was locked. I held up my gun and he nodded. We changed places. I put four shots in around the lock.

The gun gave the faintest of sighs, the wood splintered and Tucker coughed loudly to cover the noise. We didn't want the whole house in on us. Nevertheless I could hear the bullets going into the floor with loud smacks on the other side. Pieces of wood flew all over the corridor and the air was suddenly full of choking dust. Down below there came an angry rapping on the ceiling. There was still no reaction from inside the room. Tucker came over to my side.

He sort of leaned against the door. It held and then gave with a loud crack. He heeled it open quickly and flattened himself against the wall. From where I was standing I could see the corner of a table with crockery and the remains of a meal on it. My bullets had ploughed across the floor before embedding; the lino was scored and scorched and the holes the bullets made had converged, ending with a floor board, splintered and pocked reared on end. The Smith-Wesson did a lot of damage at close range.

We went through the door in a rush, fanning out each side in the gloom. Nothing moved except the blind in the faint breeze. Then there was a crash and a tinkle—I felt a needle scratch along my spinal cord. We turned round. The door-lock had fallen out of the wood and spilled over the floor. It still didn't quiet my nerves. There was something damn funny about that room. There came an angry rapping from down below. Then a voice like the siren of the *Queen Mary* floated up the stairwell. I drifted out on to the landing. The janitress was standing in the hall, glaring upwards. I resisted a temptation to spit.

"Sorry, ma'am," I said. "Hire purchase agents."

She grunted. For a minute I thought she was coming up, but the stairs were too much. She went back in and slammed the door. I went back into the apartment, shut the door behind me and wedged it with a chair. Tucker had disappeared. I went through an open door and found a small kitchen. Tucker was looking thoughtfully out the window down into a back area. A fly couldn't have got out that way. There were two doors leading off the kitchen. I opened the nearest one, slid my gun barrel round the corner and eased myself through. The room was used as a bedroom.

There was a mess of soiled sheets in one corner, stripped off an old frame bed; old fashioned wall paper, a frosted glass panel let into the window near the bed to blot out the brick wall of the area opposite. It only succeeded in being depressing. There was something else about the room too, but it took me a minute or so to locate it. Then I saw an ashtray on top of the dresser. There was a cigarette stub in the tray. It was still smoking.

A muscle fretted in my cheek. I could suddenly smell death in the room. There was no sound but the noise of a truck starting up, a long way across the block; that, and the faint slurring of a train, about a couple of miles off. It carried in the warm air. There was only one place in the room where anything could be concealed and that was the other side of the bed. I took a step around and then stopped.

No matter how many times it happens, you never get used to it. There was a black shoe sticking out from underneath the heap of bed linen. I didn't have to see the built-up heel to know who it belonged to, but I had to make sure. I didn't like touching the bedding with my bare hands, so I used the silencer on the gun barrel. The sheets parted smoothly, then fell away crimson and I was looking into the face of Captain Jacoby.

He looked surprised and very dead. Blood was still pumping from a big hole in his chest and the bullet had done a lot more damage coming out the other side. Jacoby's face looked almost as astonished as Tucker's. Neither of us said anything for a minute. A fly buzzed loudly in the silence and then settled on Jacoby's head. I didn't like that and flicked it off.

4

He still wore the brown suit and maroon socks. I fished in my pocket and presently came up with my piece of broken tooth. I went over to Jacoby and tucked it down into his breast pocket. I felt better after that.

Tucker grunted. "Damn silly thing to do," he said. He reached down for the piece of tooth, walked over to the window and flung it into the area. He stood glaring moodily through the glass.

"This'll stir up the Press. And the Commissioner," he said savagely.

"Don't tell me you mind," I said mildly.

"About him?" he said. "No, it's not that, it's just that people like Jacoby get honest cops a bad name."

I remembered what Margaret Standish had said about things being lost in pigeon holes and what Horse Jarvis, the drunk in the tank downtown had been telling me about Jacoby. We were slow, of course, wasting time, but we had some excuse. It had been quite a moment finding Jacoby; then we had the good cards in the pack—no one could get out of the building, because there wasn't a fire escape, we commanded the only door.

The cigarette might have belonged to Jacoby; whoever killed him probably used a silencer because no one seemed to have been disturbed and we heard nothing on the way up; the blood still flowing meant that the killer either had to be still in the apartment or else he had been an Olympic sprinter to get away in the time. We both had the same idea at the identical moment. We went at the kitchen door at a fast lick. The second door leading off the kitchen was locked.

I went gum-shoeing silently back into the main room. The chair wedged against the door hadn't been disturbed so no one had gone out. Anyway, I did what I should have done at first and tried all the doors and lockers in the apartment. There was nothing else in the place, only a few clothes and odds and ends. There was no other entrance and the doors led only into closets and storage space. There wasn't even a phone anywhere and the toilet wasn't big enough to house Toulouse-Lautrec. We went back into the kitchen and stared at the other door.

I knelt down and peered through the keyhole. Corny, I know and if anyone had been the other side he could have blown my head off. I could just see a dimly lit room beyond when I heard a scrabbling noise inside. I rolled aside as Tucker went at the door like an Aberdeen Angus in a lounge suit. No lock could have taken that sort of punishment and this was a flimsy affair. The door gave a shriek of protest and Tucker went through in a thunder of arms and legs.

I followed in a rush and blinked in the half-light. Nothing moved. I snapped on a switch. A bulb balefully competed with the light straggling in from behind long, thick curtains. Then there came a scrabbling again; I felt that slight tickling along the back of my neck. There was only one place it could be. Tucker padded silently over to a thick hessian curtain which blocked one window. He ripped it back and levelled his gun.

There was a sort of alcove. A man was half-seated in it. He had a sweat-soaked face and he had been trying to force up an old, distorted window frame with a kitchen knife.

He had raised it perhaps three inches before it had become hopelessly jammed. Not two feet beyond was the rusted balustrade of the only fire escape on this side of the building.

"You'd better come on out—you're only wasting your time," said Tucker, almost gently.

Paul Mellow shrugged with a defeated gesture, dropped the knife and followed us into the room. He looked a beaten man.

5

"I told you to stay away from amateurs," I said. He sat in a cheap kitchen chair and looked at us with a yellow face. Tucker's was set like concrete.

"You know this is a gas chamber job," he said, jerking his thumb through the bedroom door. Mellow licked his lips and his pupils showed white all round.

"It was nothing to do with me," he almost whispered. "I told them they'd never get away with it."

"We know about Sirocco," I told him. "He'll be picked up in time. It's the others who interest us. Who's in back of this?"

"You've got to believe me," said Mellow. "I know nothing about it. I just drive the car, get my money regularly."

"If you're in the clear how come you hang out in a crumby joint like this?" said Tucker.

"It was Johnny's idea," said Mellow. "This was just a contact place. I had to meet them here twice a week or collect mail and get my instructions."

He gave Tucker his address; a fairly high-priced hotel over on Alameda Avenue. Tucker wrote it down. Then he went to phone. Mellow looked at me appealingly.

"They will believe me, won't they. . . ?" His voice tailed off. I tried to look sympathetic. I don't do it very well and it wasn't successful.

"You could help by levelling with the Captain," I said. "If it helps any I've been retained by your brother to try and keep you out of trouble. But now. . . ." I shook my head. The act was going over great. His face lit up.

"Mandy?" He gripped my arm. "I might have guessed. He won't let me down. He always was a good guy."

"Too good for a cheap punk like you," I told him. "Only chance you've got is to turn State's. Then we may be able to do something."

The hopeless look came back into his face. "I can't do that. I ain't got much choice. Go to the gas chamber legally, or get rubbed out unofficially. It all adds up to the same thing. Either way, it don't help me none."

I sighed. "Let's skip the rest for a minute. Whoever killed Jacoby can't have been gone long. Let's assume that Jacoby was working in with Sirocco, tipping them off about police information, that sort of thing. He got a cut, same as you. The boys got tired and finished him off and left you to pay the bill."

Mellow's eyes flickered. I felt pretty sure this was the truth and kept on at him.

"Whoever put the big chill on him left only a few minutes ago."

Mellow looked up from the chair. "I don't see how you could have missed him. He must have passed you in the hall."

That made me think but it would have to wait for a bit. Tucker came back in the room. We sat down and watched Mellow. He sat and watched us.

6

The howl of prowl-car sirens was still splitting the air. Boots were thundering on the stairs, big cops cursed at the heat and the height, flash-bulbs were popping.

Said Tucker, "For Chrissake keep those reporters out." A voice echoed down the stair well. "All right, boys, you'll get all the news at the four-thirty conference."

In the kitchen Mrs. Five-by-Five was going over Paul Mellow's history, molecule by molecule, between crocodile tears. She peered over my shoulder into the bedroom. Jacoby's feet were visible and the fingerprint boys were dusting all round.

"The poor captain . . . he's dead?" she asked me.

"He'll get used to it," I said.

"He'll have to," said Tucker. The door opened and Mac-Namara came in. He looked at me with a tired expression.

"You again," he said.

"I got the T.V. rights," I said. He looked at me sharply and went on in. He took a white coat out of his bag and went to work. I went out in the hall and used the pay phone. I got Mandy Mellow.

"Faraday. You'd better come on over," I told him. I filled him in on the details. He thanked me and rang off. I went on back to the kitchen. The din was worse, if anything; Mellow sat in the chair. Tucker had been joined by two other detectives and they were taking it in turns to question him. Mc-Giver was there, too, standing in the background. He nodded at me.

"Looks like you got yourself a new boss," I said.

"Looks like it," he said. He didn't sound too tragic about it.

I went into the hall. Just one more flight up the stairs ended in a landing. There were some wooden steps up and then a wood and frosted glass door with a rusted lock. The key was in the lock. The door led to a small floored area surrounded by green painted iron railings.

There was washing waving languidly in the heavy atmosphere and evidence of other things too, but what the hell, it was fresh air. I stood over in the corner, in the lee of a chimney stack and stared away through the heat haze to the freight yards and the shimmer of L.A. beyond. Presently I saw a glimmer of light about a quarter of a mile away and then a brilliant scarlet roadster hove into view; it threaded the blocks like some enormous beetle shining in the sun and stopped almost directly underneath me. Mandy Mellow had arrived.

7

I sat in the passenger seat of the scarlet Caddy and waited for Mandy to come out; there was a battery of controls that wouldn't have disgraced the flight deck of a DC8 and the only thing missing was a T.V. screen. I wondered idly why Paul Mellow hadn't just followed along in his brother's shadow. All he had to do was shovel up the greenbacks as fast as they came over the tables; it was like printing your own money. Then I saw Mandy Mellow coming.

"How did you make out?" I asked him. He gave me a thin smile as he climbed into the driving seat. He held out his hand. "Many thanks," he said. "I owe you a lot, Faraday."

He smoked silently, flipping his used match stick in a moody arc over the windshield.

"I think we might do a deal," he said finally. He wrote me a cheque on a sort of folding desk which came down out of the dashboard. I wouldn't have been surprised to see a typewriter pop out of a cubbyhold too. The cheque was about five times what the job was worth but I took it. There wasn't anything to say.

He turned towards me. He had put on a pair of dark glasses and it was impossible to make out the expression of his eyes.

"I know very little, you understand," he said. "I knew Paul was running around with Sirocco. No one, but no one, knows where he hangs out. He comes and goes; it's my belief that he's from out of town and just flies in and out for specific jobs."

"Like Murder Incorporated?" I said. He didn't like that. He threw his cigarette butt into the gutter. One of the kids playing around the car picked it up and started to smoke it. He was all of ten years old.

"There's only one thing I know and it may have nothing to do with it," he said. "But both Paul and Sirocco sometimes had a biggish negro with them. I only saw him twice—both times at the Inn and then only for a few minutes together. But it might make things easier."

I gave Mellow a long look. Something was beginning to stir down in my memory.

"Well," I said. "Thanks, Mandy. You might have hit on something at that."

"Anything to help the kid," he said. He started the engine. The Caddy shuddered and the engine rose to a chortle as he engaged the gears. The seat hit the small of my back as the tyres gripped and we gunned off across town. I got him to drop me in front of my block. I thanked him and he drove off. Apart from a brief appearance in court and a casual drink later, that was the last I saw of him. I went over to a kiosk and got an *Examiner*. Black type about a foot deep screamed all over the front page; POLICE CHIEF JACOBY SLAIN BY UNKNOWN GUNMAN it said. GAMBLER'S BROTHER HELD IN D.A.'S PROBE. After all that there was about ten lines of the actual story at the bottom of the page, most of that wide of the mark.

I took about seventeen seconds to read the piece. I felt I had wasted my money. In the stop press I saw another fudge of blurred type, "Private investigator Michael Faraday of this city is assisting Captain Tucker in his inquiries." At least that was accurate. I went on into the building and rode up in the neolithic lift.

"Hullo," said Stella. "Another country heard from." She wore a sort of cream costume which set off her figure to perfection and she made quite a picture as she bent over the coffee percolator.

"I should stay around the office more often," I told her.

"Huh?" she said, wrinkling her nose.

"It would take too long to explain," I said. I went on over to the desk. It had a lot of paper and stuff on it, some unopened bills, one or two letters; nothing extraordinary. Stella had filed most of the stuff already, I knew. If there was anything important, she would tell me.

I went on towards her. She intercepted my sweeping hand and guided it gently back to my side. Her fingers were cool on mine and she held my hand just a fraction of a second too long. I got out Mandy Mellow's cheque and held it up for her to read. Her eyes widened.

"Yum," she said. "Looks like we'll be in business next week after all."

The phone rang. Stella handed it to me. It was Tucker. "Just thought you'd like to know," he said. "The same gun." I should have been surprised otherwise. Stella was at the other phone taking notes.

"You heard anything from the Channing girl?" Tucker asked. I said I hadn't.

"She's done nothing unusual, so far as I can see," he said. "That's what worries me."

It was my turn to grin. "She may be quite an innocent party," I said. "Anyway, she's my problem. I'll keep you posted."

He rang off. I sat back at the desk, swivelled my chair and feathered smoke up at the ceiling. It rose swiftly in the warm air and formed a fog, hiding the crumby state of the décor. I stopped torturing my mental processes and picked up my cup of coffee. There was always tomorrow.

Then I remembered something else. I had left my car over at Police H.Q. It wasn't much good locking a convertible and I had left the key in the dash pocket. I sighed again. I got Stella to ring up Police H.Q. I spoke to the desk sergeant.

"Are you still staking out my place?" I asked him after I told him who I was.

"Captain Tucker's orders," he said. "Any complaints?"

"On the contrary," I said. "Never more welcome. I just wondered if your night squad had gone on yet."

"Two men going out about half past six," he said.

I asked if one of them could take my car out for me and told him where to find the key.

"This ain't no Yellow Cab Company," he grumbled.

"Many thanks, Sergeant, for your co-operation," I said sweetly. That took him by surprise.

"Not at all, Mr. Faraday," he said. "That's a different matter. Pleased to do it."

Stella was still smiling when I came up for my second cup of coffee.

9

Bert Dexter

NEXT MORNING I showered, and had breakfast under the friendly eyes of the two cops. Margaret Standish rang. She sounded worried.

"Sorry to bother you, Mike," she said. "Someone tried to break into my apartment last night. Can you come over some time?"

I did my best to cheer her up. "I'll look around for a chat later," I told her.

Next I rang Dan Tucker. I didn't tell him about Margaret's call. It might have had nothing to do with Adrian Horvis but it was decidedly interesting.

"Paul Mellow's been booked and appears in court again formally day after tomorrow. We may want you then. Meantime, we're still digging."

I smoked and held the earphone against my shoulder and stared out of the window at the trees opposite; already it was hot enough to make them shimmer in the early haze. It was really only around eight by the sun. Then Tucker said, "You still there?"

"Sorry, Dan," I said.

He snorted. "Look, I've got to go out to the Horvis place again. Can you meet me there around ten?"

"Suits me," I said and hung up. When I went out to the

Buick the *tonneau* was red-hot from the glare of the sun. I took off my jacket, laid it on the seat alongside me and put on a pair of sunglasses. The heat of the cushions frizzled my buttocks when I sat down; I half rose and the cop leaning against my porch grinned.

"Hot seat," he said. I gunned out of the car-port, turned down the boulevard and drove across town. The day was a glaze of light and the sun struck the car bonnet and came back at my face like it was a stove-lid; I drove slowly, not from choice, but because the speed made no difference to the temperature of the air and the faster I went the quicker the insects, dust and smuts gathered in the driving seat.

I wasn't in any hurry so I stopped at Jinty's on the way over and had an iced beer; I was afraid the bar-tender was going to say "Hot" again. In which case I should have screamed. Fortunately, he was too busy to do more than put the long glass down, take the money and turn away. This brought the wheel full circle. It was less than a week ago when I had first been in here on the morning Adrian Horvis had rung me, but it seemed like a couple of years. There was no one I knew in the bar, so I came on out, got into the Buick and drove across town.

I had trouble getting on to Highway 44 what with the snarl-up of mid-morning traffic but I made better time when I hit the highway. It was a relief, though, when I got on to the dirt road and up into the hill country. It was a little cooler here, but still nothing to write to Congress about. I passed the Jazz Inn which had the usual clutter of cars choking the parking lot, found the Avocado-Peartree intersection and was on the boulevard once again.

There seemed to be one or two properties for sale since I was up here last and I noticed idly that the house next to 2168 was up for rent. The Horvis place looked even bigger than when I last saw it. I got up the marble steps with a heavy increase in my blood-rate. I knew Tucker was there because his car was parked at the bottom of the steps. The same Filipino house-boy I had seen before answered my ring.

His smile of recognition was genuine. I went on across the hall and through the *patio* and into the lounge. Tucker was sitting at Horvis's desk going through piles of paper. He gave me a silent wave of greeting.

"I get you drink, sir," said the Filipino and went off. I heard the welcome chink of glass and ice a moment later. I went and sat gratefully on one of the divans and rested my smoking feet. I guessed the Filipino was glad of something to do now that his master had gone and that set me wondering what Horvis's estate planned to do about the house; I supposed the staff had been kept on in the interim to prevent the place from running down.

Tucker grunted and spun an apple-core through the air. It hit the waste basket squarely and disappeared. The Filipino came back and set down a long glass in front of me; it was frosted, ice clinked in it and there was the smell of crushed limes. I took a tentative sip and decided this was one of the better days. Tucker thanked the house-boy and he withdrew. He seemed to go out on rubber castors for you never heard or saw him until he was on top of you. He would have made a great skating champion—without skates.

Tucker rubbed his hands. "We got it going, that's for sure. All bullets matching; Mellow set for trouble unless something turns up; Sirocco identified and a net out. Yeah, Mike, it ain't turned out at all badly."

"Except that we don't know what the hell it's all about," I said. He shrugged.

"You can't have everything," he said. I leaned back and studied my socks thoughtfully. They were a nice shade of puce. Stella had picked them out for me.

"Are you going to be long?" I asked. "Because if so, I'll take a stroll round the grounds."

He looked surprised. "Am I boring you?"

"No, it's not that," I said. "You'll get on a lot quicker and the walk will do me good."

"Right," he said. I went over to the garden porch on the opposite side of the house from the conservatory. I thought I might make it but I heard the scrunch of his teeth biting into another apple just before I went through the door. If ever a man ought to live to be a hundred it was him.

I had a walk round the garden; it was quite a sizeable affair; arbours, ornamental fountains, a gazebo, a Japanese garden, the lot. Then I strolled over to a terrace and looked down towards the garden of the empty house next door. The chauffeur was working on one of Horvis's cars; they really glistened in the sun. Then I stopped; I looked again to make sure and bells began to chime. You really do need your brains testing, Faraday, I told myself.

I went back across the lawn with great strides. I must have made a lot of noise going in through the side entrance and Tucker looked up in surprise.

"Have you got the chauffeur's name?" I asked him. He rooted among the papers on the desk.

"Eugene Lockhart," he said. "Been with the old man about seven years."

"Would you mind having him in?" I asked. I saw a funny look in his eye.

"This isn't the sun," I told him. "Just ask him a question or two, to make it look natural. I've got a wild idea, but if I'm right this will be the biggest break so far."

I'd never seen Tucker so excited, but something about me must have impressed him for he went out of the room with surprising speed and a minute later I saw the Filipino pass the window. Tucker rejoined me and sat down at the desk again.

We waited perhaps five minutes and then there was a crunching of gravel. A tall figure in a grey livery appeared at the window. There was a tap and the chauffeur walked in. As he took off his cap I saw that he was bald; his eyes blinked nervously behind pince-nez. Anyone less like a chauffeur I never saw.

"Come in, Mr. Lockhart," Tucker said. He shuffled some papers on his desk. "You were asking about that other car of Mr. Horvis's we were holding. If you'd like to come down to H.Q. this afternoon you can bring it back."

E

"Thank you, sir," said Lockhart. He nodded at me, smiled nervously at Tucker and went back out the same way he came in.

"And that's the chauffeur?" I said.

Tucker looked blankly at me. "Sure it's the chauffeur," he said. "We questioned him half a dozen times——"

"I didn't mean that," I said. "He's a white man."

"Is there any law against that?" Tucker exploded.

"Sorry," I said. "I keep forgetting. What I'm trying to get at is this. The chauffeur I saw when I was here the afternoon Horvis was killed was a negro."

I started walking rapidly up and down. Tucker opened his mouth once or twice, but no words came. He got a packet out of his pocket and lit a cigarette. "In other words——" he began.

"The murderer," I said. "It's got to be."

Tucker offered me a cigarette. I took it and put it to my mouth. I walked up and down as I spoke, pulling my thoughts together.

"Horvis was due to be hit," I said. "The trigger man—whom we'll suppose is an out-of-town gunman—happens to be a negro, which is incidental. He and Sirocco have the place staked out. The regular chauffeur has the afternoon off—we can check that later—or perhaps he's gone out for a short while. The trigger man, dressed as a chauffeur, turns up and is reconnoitring the place when I arrive.

"With commendable nerve this party starts to clean down one of the cars. Later on, he sees me out in the conservatory, seizes his chance, nips in and murders Horvis. Then he and Sirocco take off in the hire car; perhaps the negro is dropped round the corner, having changed out of his uniform meantime, and then Sirocco takes the car back to the hire firm."

There was a long silence. Tucker leaned back at the desk and took a thoughtful and lethal bite at another apple. I sipped my drink.

"Pretty good," said Tucker. "I can see one or two snags, though. Wouldn't it be taking rather a chance? The servants, for instance?"

"We've seen how these boys operate," I said. "Nothing fazes them. If anyone had seen him, or the servants had opened the door while he was in the garden, he could easily have made up some errand. It's not unusual for some of these rich old birds to send their chauffeurs out to collect a car or something of that sort. He could have said he had mistaken the address."

Tucker furrowed up his face. He threw his apple core away and took up his cigarette.

"But I still don't get it," he said. "Not that I think you haven't got something important here. Why a negro? Could anything be more conspicuous?"

"Let's tackle it from another angle," I said. "Did you ever read a story by an English guy named Chesterton? It was about this man who committed a perfect murder. Nobody saw him because he was so conspicuous. He was disguised as the postman and he carried out the body in a sack under the eyes of the police."

"So?" queried Tucker.

"So what I'm saying is this," I said. "Look at the position of the negro in this country today; they're everywhere; everywhere and nowhere. Yet do you ever see them as individual people? Can you ever say you recognize their faces? Aren't they all the same to the average white man?"

There was another long silence. I started walking again. "The fact that this gunman is a negro is purely incidental, I'd say. What's the decisive factor it that he must be one of the best men in the business; fearless, ruthless, with nerves that don't shake under stress. He's efficient at his job—apart from the shot he took at me, I don't know anyone else who survived; he killed cleanly always—except for Braganza, and that was in the dark—usually with one shot and faded away so quickly that only one or two people in all these killings gained a vague impression that a negro had been in the neighbourhood.

"And, in a variety of menial disguises, he could come and go in a hundred places without being spotted; he could mingle with waiters in a hotel and never be noticed. With Sirocco as his finger man he couldn't go wrong. Then all he has to do is get on a bus or a plane and turn up a couple of thousand miles away."

Tucker whistled. His face had changed as I was speaking. He put his hand on my shoulder.

"Not bad, Mike," he said. "It was 'The Invisible Man'."

"What do you mean?" I said.

"That story," he said.

"That was Wells," I said.

"Chesterton too," he said.

"I didn't know you could read," I said. I went over and finished my drink.

"What I can't understand," Dan said, "is why you didn't spot this sooner."

"Well," I said, "this is the sort of thing they rely on. This guy's action was an inspired piece of impromptu. He seized his chance and got away with it. I had no way of knowing whether Horvis had a coloured chauffeur or not. I just assumed so, when I saw him cleaning that car, which was what he was banking on."

Then I remembered something else Paul Mellow had said. It made me think a minute.

"Do you remember that negro who passed us in the lobby when we went out to see Mellow?" I said. "And do you remember what Mellow told us? It was something about the killer having gone such a short while before that he didn't know how we could have missed him. Well, we didn't."

A fly buzzed loudly in the sudden silence. Tucker mopped his face. "Crize," he said. "I think the sooner we nail this goon the better."

We drove down to H.Q. soon after. We went into Tucker's office, he had some coffee sent up and then he got out the slide projector. It didn't take long. I had a hunch about this too. He had a tired-looking sergeant bring in a stack of files and photostat record cards.

"Do you remember those pictures you showed me of Sirocco?" I asked him. "Can I see them again?"

I had been right, but the whole story took a little longer to sort out. We looked at a few pictures and then I asked him to stop. It was the shot of Sirocco and the group of cons in the prison courtyard. But now it was the picture of the negro in the background that interested me. It was curious to think that the last time I had looked at this, I had studied only Sirocco and hadn't given the negro a second glance. Now I dismissed Sirocco and had eyes only for the negro. That didn't tell me much; no detail.

But Tucker had a couple of men on the San Quentin files and after an hour we narrowed down the search to two men. The second set of pictures hit the jackpot. They were of an expressionless-looking negro with flat, unstaring eyes and a wide, slit-like mouth; I could recognize in it, grainy as it was, the man I had seen in chauffeur's uniform at the Horvis place, but it had been too dark in the hall of the apartment house for me to place him. I put my finger on the stack of glossies. Tucker gave me a curt nod, but his eyes had a glint to them. I looked at the photostat record card when it came up. It was a good record if you counted crime in plus-units. From petty larceny, assault and unlawful wounding it progressed to full-scale murder.

His name was the grandiloquent one of Napoleon Latour Jones. Alias "Buck" Jones, alias Charles Jackson and about a dozen more. He had served ten years on one capital charge, reduced to six for good behaviour. Born in New Orleans, his jail sentences overlapped Sirocco's at San Quentin by two years; there was the link between them.

I leaned back in the chair and drank my second cup of coffee. I was beginning to feel as much at home in Tucker's office as my own. I wondered if I shouldn't make him an offer towards the rent. Tucker had some teleprinter messages sent off. Half an hour later he had some more information.

"Goes under the name of Charlie Jackson now," he said. "That's something."

I sat it out with him for another hour or so and then thought I'd better blow; it was already gone one and I'd done only half the things I intended. Though the day hadn't been at all bad.

"See you later," said Tucker. "I gotta burn the wires up. Thanks again."

"Call me if anything urgent turns up," I said. When I drove off I made a few turns into side streets and kept my eyes peeled in the mirror; no reason really, and there was no ground for thinking I might be tailed, but I had an idea things would get hotter than the weather in a couple of days.

I was pretty sure the artist with the gun would stick around to see what turned up at the Paul Mellow trial and I was certain that the end of the string, whatever it was, would be found in L.A. Though the heat haze, smog and my dark glasses made observation difficult I could see nobody behind so I stopped playing games and drove over by the straight route. It was still a roaster and the shop was open, I could see, as I drew up underneath the sun-blind.

The door was propped back with a brass ornament, which saved me the carillon when I went in. Though I walked silently on the thick rug, Margaret Standish had seen me coming, for she suddenly appeared at the back of the *salon*. I supposed she must have a mirror somewhere in the office. It may have been imagination but I thought she looked a little pale and drawn.

I followed her into a small office, panelled in sapele and soft-woods; in contrast to the shop, everything was modern. There was a red plastic phone, a bright green German typewriter on a table with tubular steel U legs, grey metal filing cabinets and a Swedish paper lampshade on the flush-sunk ceiling light. The only concession to the past was the carpet, which was plain grey but thick and very, very expensive.

She sat down at the desk with a sudden shirring of sheer stockings and smoothed her skirt. "It's been a long time," she said.

"All of three days," I said. She laughed suddenly; perhaps more from nervous strain than good humour, showing fine teeth.

"What have you found out?" she said.

"You know all about Jacoby?" I said.

"I read the papers," she said.

"All linked up," I said. "Johnson, Braganza, Adrian Horvis, Jacoby and the boy who took a shot at me—bullets match, everything."

She went white and her hands trembled. "I had no idea," she said. She fumbled in the desk drawer and came up with a cigarette packet.

"Take it easy," I said. "Things are clearing up. We've identified the men responsible and now it's only a question of time." I held out a match and she lit the cigarette.

"Thank God," she said, between puffs. "This is beginning to get me down. And then this business last night. . . ."

"You must tell me about this," I said.

"Nothing to tell, apart from what I said then," she said. "I disturbed somebody at the door and that was it. I phoned the police and they sent somebody over. Anyway, the officer who came, Mr. McGiver, seemed very capable. He had a look round and said I'd be hearing from him."

I was glad it had been McGiver; Tucker had told me he had had him transferred to H.Q. from Jacoby's goon squad.

"We'd better have a look at that door," I said.

We went outside and up the staircase. At the main entrance I bent down and examined the door. The lock plate was all scarred and scratched; a piece of wood about two inches long had been gouged from the woodwork, evidently where the instrument being used—something like a cold chisel—had slipped. And there was further splitting on the edge of the door, where the chisel had been inserted to get additional leverage. From a cursory glance it looked exactly like my own front door after the night visit, but I didn't tell Margaret that.

"What do you think, Mike?" she asked. I rubbed my chin.

"I shouldn't worry," I said. "I'll ask Tucker to keep an eye on you at night. Another week or so should see things cleared up."

"I'd rather you do that," she said.

"Do what?" I said.

"Keep an eye on me at night," she said.

"It's the hot weather," I told her.

She was standing at the top of the steps; she was wearing a white dress with blue polka dots and she hadn't got on her glasses. The sun was strong and it shone clear through the thin material of the dress. She had only underpants and a bra about two inches wide underneath. They were peach-coloured. I didn't have to guess that. The sun sure was strong that afternoon.

The sight of her standing there stopped me in my train of thought. She stayed there, sort of pirouetting, one hand shading her eyes against the light. Her legs were pretty statuesque and she wore black velvet stiletto-heeled shoes. I thought to myself if I took as much notice of the facts of my cases when I was working, I would make Sherlock Holmes look like a two-bit amateur, However, like a lot of things, this set-up would have to be left for the time being.

She must have read my thoughts anyway, for she chuckled abruptly and went down the steps. She sounded pretty pleased with herself. I was feeling pretty randy to tell the truth, but it was as hot as hell and I had a lot of things to do. When we got back into the office I gave her some good advice about keeping the phone by her bed and making sure the alarm was on the door; I didn't really think she was in any danger now. I had got it in my head that Sirocco and his dark chum were after that key.

I was pretty certain, though, that they wouldn't kill again in L.A. unless it was absolutely imperative. Even they had stuck at eliminating Paul Mellow, though it would have been easy to do, and with the newspapers screaming the Jacoby killing all over town they were sure to hole up for a bit unless they were prodded into the open. I figured it was up to Tucker and me to do that prodding; to make them break out, and it had to be something to do with the key.

"Right," I said. "I'm away. I'll let you know what happens."

She saw me to the door. I waved from the driving seat, edged into the traffic and drove across town.

2

The Chase National Bank was a big pink granite building on one of the main intersections of L.A. It looked too grand to deal with anything so sordid as money and the resplendent commissionaire in the main concourse evidently shared that view. At any rate he eyed me up and down as though I had a bad case of fallen bank-rate. The manager was in, fortunately.

A woman with a square figure, orange cardigan and a face to match showed me through into a wall-to-wall carpeted hall. We stopped in front of a mahogany door; on it was stencilled in pale yellow the legend : OGILVY L. WHIPPLEBY.

"I don't believe it," I told the girl. She goggled anxiously and then suppressed a giggle.

"Come in," a mellifluous voice boomed from inside. St. Peter couldn't have worked reception better at the Pearly Gates. I went on in. There was about three acres of carpet; way off in the distance I could see a desk, set in front of frosted glass panelling. When I got up to the desk that was about an acre wide too.

Seated in back was an enormously tall man dressed in a blue pinstripe with a pale blue bow tie. He had a face like a frightened camel, long and lean, with receding white hair. He was leaning back in a brown leather and steel arm-chair making with the papers like he was busy.

"Please sit down," he said, waving me towards a chair in front of the desk. This was steel and wood and uncomfortable too; probably to discourage visitors from staying to ask for an overdraft.

"What can I do for you, Mr. . . . er. . . ."

"Faraday," I said. I handed over my P.I. licence. His eyes widened.

"Well, Mr. Faraday," he said. "You've been having a busy time lately. Haven't I been reading something about you in the papers?"

"You have," I said. "I'd like some co-operation if you'd be so good."

"I'd be glad to help if I can," he said. "Might I ask if this has any connection with these terrible things I see in the papers?"

"I'm afraid you may not," I said. "My business is highly confidential, Mr. Whippleby, just as yours is. Suppose I came in and asked you for details of a customer's financial standing?"

"Quite so, Mr. Faraday, quite so," he said hastily. "You must forgive me. I shouldn't have asked you that, of course."

He had quite the plummiest voice I ever heard. "Just what is it I can do for you, Mr. Faraday?"

I threw the key on to his desk. "I'd like to open the box that belongs to," I said. "Perhaps you'd like to have the contents brought here or could I open it myself?"

He said nothing but took the key. He examined it and then got up and crossed to a set of filing cabinets in one corner. He was about six feet seven when he stood up and he walked like he was trying to hold a pea between the cheeks of his ass. He came back with a small ledger and sat down again. He ran his finger down a column.

"Ah, here we are. Mr. Horvis. Oh, dear, the will hasn't been read yet, I believe."

"I have the beneficiary's permission," I said.

"Mrs. Standish," he said. "I understand, quite unofficially you know, that she will inherit. It's a mere technicality, but still. . . ."

"If you have any doubts, Mr. Whippleby," I said, indicating the phone. "I've just come from her place."

He relaxed. "That won't really be necessary, Mr. Faraday. I like to help where I can. As long as you're sure there won't be . . . shall we say . . . any difficulties?"

"Absolute discretion, Mr. Whippleby," I said.

"Ah, that's grand," he said in that plummy voice. "Very good. In that case there's no need for further delay."

He pressed a button and a buzzer sounded somewhere. He spoke into an intercom. "Miss Gorlinsky? Will you come in a moment, please?"

A short while later the door opened and the square job in the orange sweater wheeled in. Whippleby spoke to her in muffled tones and handed her the key. She turned to me.

"Will you come this way, Mr. Faraday, please?" They were laying the courtesy on with a trowel. Whippleby held out his hand. I took it. It was cool and firm.

"Many thanks, Mr. Whippleby," I said.

"Not at all," he said smoothly. "Only too pleased." He was already miles away. I followed Miss Gorlinsky through a door at the rear of Whippleby's office and down another corridor. Here we waited while an attendant unlocked a door and let us through; he locked it again behind us. We went along another corridor and into an office furnished with functional furniture and a desk. Here I signed a paper which Miss Gorlinsky put in a drawer; we went through another door and into a sort of vault. This place made the Bastille seem like open house. The room was lined with green-painted steel lockers. Miss Gorlinsky took me down several aisles and then handed me the key.

We stopped in front of a locker in the fourth tier. It had the letters 791 painted on it in white. I must say it was quite a moment when I put the key in the lock and turned it; when I lifted the steel doorflap downwards I saw there was another steel box inside the locker, compeltely filling it. This had a steel handle in the middle of it and when I pulled this the whole thing lifted out; it was about the same size as a wine-crate, but not quite so heavy.

"Will you follow me, please?" said Miss Gorlinsky. We walked about another three miles between the lockers; she left the door of 791 open. Presently we came to another small office; this was comfortably furnished, with a large table, easy chairs, a telephone and a good carpet. I put down the box on the table with some relief. Miss Gorlinsky handed me a piece of paper and went out.

"Please ring if you need anything, Mr. Faraday," she said. "When you have finished, sound the buzzer and I will come and conduct you out."

"Thanks," I said.

She went out a second door communicating with the room and when I looked up again I could see the shadow of a guard's peaked cap against the frosted glass. It was very quiet in here, except for the faint hum of the air-conditioning from far away; it was cool too, probably the coolest place I had been in for weeks, but I was beginning to sweat.

Then I sat down at the table and pulled the box towards me; I saw that it had another lock on top of it, set in flush with the lid. This had a dial like a telephone with numbers and letters on it. Then I saw the purpose of the paper Miss Gorlinsky had left behind her. She had writen the combination on it.

I dialled the number; there was a sweet click and the next moment the top lid of the box came away in my hands. When I got it out, the whole thing came away from the hinge pivots inside and I laid it down on the table out of the way. I sat back and lit a cigarette and stared at what was in the box.

It was a battered old brown leather valise which completely filled the interior of the case. I prodded it with my finger and it felt heavy. I had already made up my mind what it was, but what it contained was another matter. If it was locked, I was sunk, but I wanted to relax for a minute or two before I went on to the next stage.

3

I was pretty sure that what I was looking at was Braganza's missing case; the case that half the police of L.A. had been searching months for. The case that might contain the solution of the whole problem. But if that were so it made my part in the affair completely pointless and forced me to revise my opinion of Horvis from top to bottom. The story about the jade ornaments had been exploded, then the motor automation plant, but I couldn't understand this angle at all.

If this was Braganza's case, then it might equally well contain the article I had been retained to recover; the case might even belong to Horvis. But why had he called me in if he had the case himself safely under lock and key? And if Braganza had been killed while carrying the case, why hadn't Sirocco, the negro gunman or the people behind them stolen it at the same time?

I lifted the case out and pushed the steel locker to one side. The valise was pretty worn, the handle was rubbed as though it had been carried many times; more to the point, it was as anonymous as a case of that sort might well be. It was neither too expensive or unduly cheap and hundreds of thousands of them were sold the length and breadth of the States.

Any hopes that Horvis or Braganza's initials might be stamped on the side of it, weak as they were, were completely dashed as I held it up. In view of what it contained the thought was as plausible as a rummy's dream of life without alcohol. However, I was in luck in one respect. The key of the valise was tied to the handle with a piece of thick twine.

There was only one but it was of rather a peculiar pattern, which would make it difficult to duplicate. It was quite impossible, as we found later, for it was a rather special valise after all. It had been heavily doctored after purchase; the lining was made of mesh steel so that it was impossible to cut it open; the contents were sealed in an opaque plastic binding; and if any attempt was made to force the lock, an alarm bell sounded and valves emitted a type of tear gas. It was fortunate I didn't have to try anything like that in the bank.

As it turned out, I merely unlocked the case, took out the plastic wrapped bundle and laid that down on the table. This was beginning to feel like the Chinese mystery puzzle. The plastic was done up with sellotape and I peeled it off, layer after layer, until the thick bundle of paper inside was revealed. I sighed, sat back at the table and started to read. The documents were mostly printed or typed. At the head of the first sheet I looked at it had printed : Atomic Energy Authority.

I read on for over an hour, my cigarette burning out unnoticed in the ash tray. There was page after page of top secret information; tables of figures and coded groups; photo-stat memos; diagrams, drawings of circuits so complicated that I didn't even begin to comprehend; directives from Government agencies and other stuff so hot that I felt the table might melt if I read on too long.

The minutes wheeled by and I finally gave up half-way through the bundle. There was enough stuff there to make me realize why four men had been murdered; their deaths began to look like chicken feed as I started to comprehend what was involved. I riffed through the paper again; the addresses, installations, factories and agencies mentioned in this pile ranged the whole country across. The implications were so serious that far more than State-wide measures would be needed; we would have to go to the top.

I lit my cigarette again. The dates on the documents covered a period of a few months and finished up—here I did some rough checking—about a week before Braganza had been killed. Though there were some pieces which needed to be filled in we now had our motive and the general pattern. The negro Jackson, Paul Mellow and Sirocco were the crudest, minute cogs in a vast network; the hammer which was con-trolled by shadowy men, obviously in positions of power and scattered throughout the country.

It was obvious why Adrian Horvis had been frightened for his life; why Braganza, his agent had been killed and I was even beginning to realize, however foggily, why I had been called in; as a front possibly, to convince desperate men that Horvis was on the level? That he hadn't betrayed his associates?

This was something I couldn't sleep on; I had to contact Tucker as soon as possible and we had to get things moving, all the way up. I looked through the papers once again. I daren't abstract any of them but I could take a note or two of the salient points. I decided to leave everything in the vault, where it would be safe and then examine the papers again with Tucker. But first I had some explaining to do.

I had picked up the papers to put them back in the plastic

cover, when I glanced at the last sheet; I couldn't make out what its rows of printed figures meant—they looked like something turned out by an electronic computer. There was just one word, scrawled faintly in pencil on the bottom. I copied it out; it was in wavering letters and looked like : CRTIS. It might have no significance but one never knew. I stashed all the stuff in the locker again and pressed the buzzer. The phone rang.

"I'm ready now, Miss Gorlinsky," I said.

4

When we had gone through the pantomime of restoring the deposit box to the vault, Miss Gorlinsky took me back to the outer office. I asked the girl for some packing paper and string. When she brought it I made up another little parcel. Then I thanked her and left. When I got outside the heat hit me like a trip-hammer. I wilted behind the wheel of the car and drove across town.

When I got to the main post office building I went on in and found an empty cubicle; I addressed the package, in ink, to Stella at her private address this time; I wrote the name and address on it several times to make sure. Then I handed it over to Uncle Sam's mail, registered it and pocketed the receipt. It was now getting on for five and judged by my standards it had been a pretty smooth day; certainly the most progressive so far as this case was concerned.

Provided I could avoid getting shot at, beaten up, flung into jail or seduced before nightfall, I should have about ten points out of ten. I reflected for a minute and then took the last item off my prohibited list. I went into a booth in the post office building and called Stella. I arranged to pick her up at the office at about seven and run her home. Then I drove over to Jinty's.

I needed time to think. I had been congratulating myself on my keenness of mind and all the time Horvis had been playing me for a sucker; well, the laugh was on him now. He hadn't dared go to the police but he had engaged me as a front. Not surprisingly, in view of the circumstances, I had jumped to a number of wrong conclusions; he had encouraged me, knowing that I was unlikely to uncover the true facts about Braganza's death.

Working from the wrong assumption in the beginning, I should have failed to tie in any of the subsequent information. That the police and other official bodies had done no better, was no consolation. But there it was. It seemed to be brewing up for a storm; it was as hot as all hell and heavy cloud was beginning to pile up the sky. I ordered an iced lager and took it over to a booth in the corner of the bar. Music was playing somewhere far off; something dreamy and Cole Porterish, and the conversation in the bar was low. I leaned against the padded seating of the booth and took a long, cold pull at the beer.

Later, I got in the car and drove on over to the office. I had a job to park, as usual and finally slotted the car in about two blocks away. It was as I began to walk back that I heard an ambulance siren screaming in the far distance. I took no par-ticular notice; sirens are always sounding off in L.A. about something.

Then, when I got to my own building I smelt trouble. The ambulance was standing outside and one or two people were looking curiously towards the entrance. I had a funny hunch as I went on in. I rode up in the elevator and went along the corridor. As I turned the corner I heard the noise of many voices; there were people packing the corridor, flash bulbs going off, blue uniforms and the occasional staccato noise of a typewriter. I pushed my way through the crowd, a certain conviction a dead weight in my stomach.

A big cop barred my way. "Sorry, mister," he said. I slipped my card at him; my mouth had gone dry all of a sudden. Faces were turned towards me. The big cop took my arm.

"This is my office," I said. I needn't have worried, he was only pushing me through. When I got the other side of the crowd there were more flash bulbs going. I could see the door

of the office now. There was a big hole drilled clean through
the middle of the frosted glass and fragments of glass were all
over the carpet. We went on in. There was a sudden hush and
the typewriter stopped clacking. The room seemed full of
people. I thought I recognized McGiver but colours and im-
pressions seemed to be going. I didn't want to ask any questions
and kept on walking.

"Says his name's Faraday," the big cop said to someone at
my elbow.

"Says this is his office." He sounded disbelieving.

I didn't know why I expected anything different but there
had to be a reason for the carnival; I took another pace forward and stopped. There was quite a lot of blood for such a
small person, I thought curiously. A policeman and two men
in plain clothes stepped back.

There was something lying in front of my desk. It was
covered in a white sheet but I had seen death too many times
to mistake that ultimate rigidity. There was something lying
the other side of the sheet, too. I didn't need to look again
to see it was Stella's handbag.

10

Uncle Tom

I STOOD stock-still. I had wondered for a long time what a moment like this might be like. Now I knew. McGiver knelt down and very gently pulled back the sheet from the face. No woman ever looked like this before. I stared for quite half a minute before comprehending.

Bert Dexter looked very surprised. His eyes were wide open and his mouth looked like he was right in the middle of a sentence when the blast caught him. There was that strange look of peace, though, like they all have. I put back the cloth myself and stood up. There was a scraping noise behind the alcove screen where we made the coffee. The two plain clothes men standing by the typewriter coughed awkwardly. Stella came towards me. Her face was whiter than white. She came into my arms without a word. I caught her and held her very close.

Over her shoulder McGiver blinked. I led Stella to the table and she sat down.

"What gives here?" said the big cop who had come in with me.

"If this guy owns the office then who's this?"

I saved him the trouble. "He was mistaken for somebody else," I said. "Whoever shot him was gunning for me. I expect he saw him through the frosted glass and as we're about the same height came to the wrong conclusion."

The big cop shook his head. "Pretty expensive mistake," he said. "Poor guy." He went on out. Stella took a cup of coffee from one of the plain clothes men and started to drink. The colour was coming back into her face. It had looked like the shade of a choir-boy's crime sheet. Now it was only off-pink.

"Bert was full of some baseball game he was going to see tomorrow," she said. "He sat down on the edge of the desk and was just saying something about how he must be getting along when there was a funny plop. Then all the glass in the door smashed in."

She stopped for a moment and took another sip of coffee.

"I ran over to the door; I should have known better, I suppose, but I didn't see any danger in it. All I heard was the lift going down. There was no one there. Then I saw Bert's feet sticking out from behind the desk. I phoned for the police and then I felt sick."

I put my hand on her shoulder and turned to McGiver. "Does Dan Tucker know?" I said.

He shook his head. "I just tried to reach him but I can't get him at the office or at home."

We sat down near Bert Dexter's desk. I could still see the same spider in the window on my side of the office. Nothing had changed; yet everything had changed. MacNamara appeared in the doorway. He stopped and blinked.

"Over there," I said.

"The cases come to you now, then," he said dryly. He went on over and pulled back the sheet. A few minutes later we left; Stella and me and McGiver, that is. I drove Stella in my car and McGiver followed in a prowl car. When we got to Stella's address, I went back to see McGiver. He sat behind with his engine running. He wound down the window.

"I think this business will blow wide open in the next few hours," I said. "If you can get hold of Tucker tell him to contact me. I'm going straight home and I'll wait for his call. It's just about top urgent. Sorry I can't tell you any more."

"That's all right," he said. "I'll get the message to him somehow. I'm on duty all night if you want me for anything."

I went back to Stella. "Ring me if you need anything," I said. We stood looking at one another. We didn't kiss, but she looked at me like she wasn't sure she was going to see me again. Then she smiled. Her step was brisk and confident as she walked towards the elevator. I went on out and drove home. On the way across town I got a paper.

The latest edition on the street was screaming Bert Dexter's murder and the police measures being taken to turn the State inside out—all the usual crap. When I got home I found two fresh cops on duty; they were brewing coffee in the kitchen and listening to the baseball reports.

"There was a phone call for you a while back," said the youngest, a slim, red-haired lad with big shoulders. "I got the number somewhere."

He produced a piece of crumpled notepaper from behind the toaster. I went on into the living-room and took off my jacket. The air was freshening a little but it was still pretty hot. Crickets were chirping outside the window and when I looked at my watch I was surprised to see it was almost nine o'clock. I put the registered package receipt in my hideout under the table; I didn't want that found on me. I drank a cup of coffee the young cop brought in and grabbed a sandwich.

He left an almost full pot on my side table and I emptied that. Afterwards I felt I might live.

I dialled the Morningdale number. As I had thought, it was a director of Gimpel's, the agency Bert Dexter worked for. We didn't start off too happily though.

"This is Adzel Q. Chote II," he said.

"That must be nice for you," I said. He spluttered. "This is a serious matter, Mr. Faraday."

"I'm sorry, Mr. Chote," I said. "But I've had a hard day. Do you mind stating your business?"

"My business, sir, concerns the dreadful affair of Mr. Dexter, one of my most highly valued employees."

"I see," I said. I sobered down after that. Put briefly the old boy wanted to sever any connection with the most highly uninsurable P.I. in L.A. Can't say I blamed him. We compromised in the end by my suggesting a division of the office into two, building another door and a dividing wall.

"Dear, dear," he bleated. "This business has caused a great deal of upset and unpleasantness at head office."

"It hasn't done Bert Dexter much good either," I told him. "Quite so, Mr. Faraday, quite so," he said. "I didn't mean to imply——"

I put the phone down on the old goat and finished my coffee. I was just getting ready to take a shower when the phone rang. I thought it might be Stella, but it was a man's voice.

"Sorry to bother you, Mr. Faraday," it said, "but this is urgent. This is Sergeant Clark down at Central H.Q. I've got a message from Captain Tucker. Have you got a pencil?"

I got one and waited.

"I gave him your message but he couldn't wait. He seemed pretty excited. He wants you to meet him as soon as you can at the old Acme Quarry Company's place over on Sunset Canyon. I expect you know the layout."

"I don't but I can soon find it," I said.

"Well," he said, "you take the old Sunset Turnpike and turn off after about seven miles and it's three miles up the side turning. The place is a cul-de-sac, so you can't overshoot. The captain said it was urgent and in strict confidence—the message is personal to you only."

"Do you know what it's all about?" I said.

The sergeant sounded amused. "Sorry, sir," he said. "The captain doesn't take me into his confidence. But he seemed awful excited about it and he said it was most important."

"When was this?" I asked.

"About half an hour ago," he said.

"O.K., Sergeant," I said. "Many thanks. I'm on my way." I put down the phone and sat smoking for a few moments. Then I went up top, checked on the Smith-Wesson, the silencer and the state of my ammunition. I put a few loose shells into the pouch of my shoulder holster. Then I went downstairs again. I frowned at the phone. I sat down and dialled the

Central Police H.Q. The grounds in the bottom of my coffee cup grinned up at me.

"Police," said a metallic voice.

"Could you tell me if you have a desk sergeant there named Clark?" I said.

"Certainly, sir," said the cop. "He's on the other phone. Can you hang on, or could I help you?"

"I'd like to speak to him personally," I said. There was a short delay and then another voice.

"Faraday here," I said. "Are you the officer who spoke to me a few minutes ago about a message from Captain Tucker?"

"Oh, yes, sir," he said. "Anything wrong? You got the address okay?"

"It's all right," I said. "Just checking." I put down the phone and said good night to the two cops. I leaned against the car and smoked. Nothing moved in the street, but farther down, a sudden freak gust of wind whirled over a piece of paper in the gutter. There was a scent of lilacs in the air, probably from one of the public parks. Driving across town I almost caught myself smiling.

2

Sunset Canyon was about fourteen miles from where I was living and I figured it was about forty minutes' drive, over the twisting roads in the dark. I stopped at a gas station on my way and filled up the tank; while I was waiting I got the large-scale map of L.A. out of my dash pocket and studied the terrain. I soon spotted the turning I wanted on the turnpike and though the quarry wasn't marked, I had no doubt that it would be where the police said it was.

I wondered what Tucker had unearthed that had sent him haring out there. It surely couldn't be the marksman's hide-out and yet it was a perfect place, nestling up in the maze of hills and canyons around L.A. Something else I had forgotten too; it was only about two miles from where Braganza's body had been found; a muscle in my cheek began to twitch.

It was a pretty warm night so I put the Buick's hood down and got the gas station attendant to sponge off the windscreen to leave the glass as clear as possible. My lights would be spotted for miles coming up the canyon road and if Tucker and his men had unearthed any ugly customers I wanted to be able to see plainly in case I had to take any evasive action. I put the car radio on and the dance music lulled me into a fine sense of security all the way across town.

The traffic was surprisingly light and the headlamp beams along the dark tarmac had partly mesmerized me when I crossed the city, so that I almost missed the turning on to the old turnpike. The road was bad and the tyres drummed on the uneven surface so that I reduced speed to a crawl. When I had gone a few hundred yards, I doused my lights, stopped and switched off the engine. All was silent except for the cigales shurring.

It was about a quarter to ten before I finally hit the turn off the turnpike; I had delayed a bit at the gas station and the trip had taken me longer than I figured. I stopped again on the secondary road; this was a lot worse than the turnpike and was really nothing more than a dirt track full of holes and gullies. I sat and listened again but nothing stirred. Then I drove on. I had to keep coasting at about five miles an hour in places as the surface flung the car all over the place. The road started to go uphill pretty steeply after about a mile and I had to change gear.

And I couldn't turn round either, I realized, for the road was too narrow, the edges fell away into steep gullies fringed with scrub and bushes. Some place for an ambush. I doused my dash lights. That way, I shouldn't make a side-target at any rate. After a few more minutes there was a hollow rumble under the wheels and I was going over some sort of metal bridge. The head beam picked up the white walls of cliffs, there were several large buildings and piles of rusting machinery.

I drove in an arc and fetched up in front of a row of sheds. The lights caught a large hoarding tilted at an angle. I saw the faded letters : Acme Quarry—the rest was eroded. I killed my lights and the motor and eased myself out of the car. I loosened the gun in my holster and got hold of a large, rubber-mounted flashlight from the dashboard; it would make a pretty hefty club in case of emergency, as well as lighting my way.

Nothing moved in all the wide world except for the tips of the grass around me in a soft night wind which had sprung up in the hills. A scratching noise set my nerves on edge, until I saw a puffball flicker along the body of the car and roll rapidly towards the sheds in the sudden breeze. The moon was brighter than I would have liked, but that couldn't be helped. I thought I'd go back off the open space into the grass and work around to where I could creep up behind some sheds. I couldn't see any sign of Tucker or his men and that way I shouldn't run into the wrong parties.

The grass was about three feet tall and surprisingly wet, considering the heat of the day. From somewhere far off an owl hooted and I stopped dead at the suddenness of the sound. Then I went on again. I had gone about two hundred yards and had worked near the out-buildings when I made out a dark shape in between me and the sheds. I gum-shoed through the grass, making at little noise as possible. When I got up close I could see that it was a large black car, parked round out of sight of the road. I eased myself on to the tarmac of the hard standing and found myself looking at one of the L.A. police prowl cars; I risked a quick flash at the number plate and saw that it was Tucker's.

Something was going on, that was for sure, or there would be lights and police in evidence. For no reason at all I decided to keep on behind the sheds. In the shadow and moving as quietly as I could I padded along, with the wall of an out-building on my right hand. Way off in back some sort of machinery was silhouetted against the night sky; presently I came to another open space. In front was a bright patch of moonlight and beyond, a large iron staircase went up to a balcony and another big building.

I covered the ground in five seconds flat. I stopped in the

shadow with my foot on the lowest rung of the staircase. The silence was unnatural and I found myself sweating. I made my way up about a millimetre at a time. It seemed like ten years before I got to the top; the damned thing kept creaking and flaking rust from the handrail was falling into the area below. The noise was probably equivalent to a feather falling three feet into cold rice, but to me it sounded like steel chain hitting a bass drum from a thousand feet.

So I lay down and went up the staircase on all fours; it was damn silly but the characters we were dealing with could knock a fly's eyelash out at fifty paces and the time for taking chances was gone. It was still quiet and I finally got to the top; the effort involved made Everest seem like an afternoon stroll on a bowling green. I eased my gun out of the holster on the way up and fanned it in front of me as I put one foot down after the other. I walked so softly it wouldn't have bruised the surface of a greengage jelly.

I found myself on a wide wooden planked platform which ran around the top of the building. It went away into the darkness for perhaps a couple of hundred feet; there were beams and gantries jutting out at the top, a line of windows and several doors. Not a light showed anywhere, but I decided to try the doors, one by one, before looking elsewhere. The owl hooted again and my nerves felt like they always do when someone slides a squeaky pencil down a slate. I eased along the platform and softly tried the handle of the first door; I put my weight against it, but it didn't budge. I tried the second without any result.

I was just moving on to the third when, with heart-stopping suddenness, a brilliant light sliced across the front of my face and chopped the boards ahead of me with harsh clarity. I felt sweat running down inside my coat. I took two quick steps to my right and flattened myself against the wall. The gun automatically came up and I transferred it to my left hand and edged along the wall with my right. I worked over to the window with infinite slowness. The interior was empty, but it looked something like the inside of a mill except that the machinery I could see was made of metal instead of flat grinding stones.

There were some rough wooden benches and crates. A single naked bulb burned in the ceiling fitting. It looked pretty dusty, like the plant hadn't been operating for years. I went down below the level of the window and made for the door. I got the door open about two inches and my doubts dropped away. There was a big wooden crate just inside. On the top of it was a single green apple-core that could have belonged to only one person. It was a beautiful sight.

I stepped inside the door and lowered my gun to look around for Tucker. It wasn't the only mistake I had made that evening, but it was the biggest and pretty nearly fatal. I found myself looking at one of the ugliest faces this side of the Chamber of Horrors. It belonged to a big, chunky-built negro with mean eyes and one of the grimmest mouths that ever came out of San Quentin. His gun was rock-steady and perfectly level; it pointed straight at my navel and I didn't have to look at the silencer to know who he was what he was or to realize that the safety-catch was off and that the bullet was a fraction of a second off my gut.

I stood perfectly still and we stared at one another for perhaps two whole seconds. He gave a sinister smile that was probably the last thing quite a number of people in L.A. had to remember on their way to the grave.

"Come on in, white trash," he said with a soft, Southern slur.

I dropped the gun at the same time as something stirred behind me. Then the top of my head exploded, cannon shells were pumping into my engine and I went down in flames into a shark-filled sea.

3

Dan Tucker looked worried. His face was red, his eyes were hot and angry. So far as I could make out he was trussed up like a Christmas parcel. He sat in the angle of some machinery and looked at me with concern. My mouth felt like the floor of a coke store and a couple of boiler makers were playing a Bach cantata with steel bars on the top of my skull. I tasted blood on the inside of my mouth. Carefully—I was worried in case the front of my face fell off—I tried to move my hands. They seemed to be tied together with something like baling wire.

"Don't try to move," said Tucker. I had just voted him Comic of the Month, when I realized he was being solicitous about my physical condition, rather than humorous about my situation.

Tucker was roped to what looked like a piece of earth-crushing machinery. We were alone but I felt that company was close at hand. I closed my eyes for a bit and when I opened them again the mist had cleared somewhat. I spat to clear my throat and it was pure blood; that could mean any-thing. I didn't like the blood from my insides. I explored with my tongue. I was relieved to find it was only a tooth which had cut the inside of my mouth. I should live—for a bit, anyway. Half an hour? An hour? I weighed it up quite dispassionately, for it was for sure that our friends Charlie Johnson and Sirocco couldn't afford to let us go. Too much was at stake for that.

I flicked my eyes at Tucker. "No cops?" I said.

"No cops," he said. "Where'd you get the call from?"

"One of your sergeants," I said. "He's probably half-way to Alaska by now."

He looked incredulous.

"Don't let's waste a lot of time on this," I told him. "A chummy fellow name of Clark. He said you wanted to see me here alone. I presume you got the same message from him, only giving my name. The oldest gag in the world."

It was obvious Dan still had no idea what I was talking about.

"We're in a tough spot," I said. "How long have we got?"

"Might be half an hour," he said. "These babies—Sirocco and the negro—are waiting for someone higher up. They obviously want to find out how much we know—before the execution."

"Sounds great," I said without enthusiasm. "Are we being watched?"

"They ain't far away," he said. "That's why I asked you not to move. I've been working on these ropes ever since I got here."

"Any luck?" I asked. He winced and I saw sweat on his forehead.

"Matter of time," he said. "But time is one thing we ain't got."

"How did they get the drop on you?" I asked.

"Simple," he said. "I expected you. Someone came out on the balcony and shouted for me to come on up. I got up the ladder. I was pretty puffed so I stood in the door——"

"And finished your apple," I said.

"Why, yes," he said without surprise. "Then the two of them came round the door and that was it. Like taking the crutches out from under a cripple."

"Just about their style, too," I said. I looked back over my shoulder. I couldn't see anything, except the corner of a door some way off.

"Listen, Dan," I said. "This is very important. Sirocco and Jones are only two noodles in a very big plate of soup. You won't see your desk sergeant again, either. He was another member of the organization."

Tucker looked up at the ceiling. He smiled very patiently.

"Involving Braganza, Horvis and the rest," he said.

"Exactly," I said. "It sounds corny, Dan, I know, but this business is on a very large scale. Leakages of information, details of war plant, atomic installations, all the way from Washington to Alaska."

Tucker's mouth sagged open. "How the hell do you know——?" he began.

I told him. This time I really levelled with him. I started right at the beginning and filled in all the holes for him. Margaret Standish, the key, the Chase National. It took about ten minutes all told—ten minutes we could ill afford, but somebody else had to be able to hold all the pieces together, though Bert Dexter's insurance company wouldn't have handled either of us. I told him about Bert too. His face was grim when I finished.

"I ought to blast you to hell and back for holding out on that key," he said. "But this is neither the time nor the place."

As he spoke I could feel my head clearing; the steam hammers were still going, but blood was coming back into my limbs and I tried flexing my arms against the bonds.

"Let me slice it this way," I said. "For argument's sake let's say this large-scale espionage system has been operating for some years."

"The Russkies?" he said.

"How would I know?" I said. "What does it matter? The Russians, the Poles, the East Germans, the Communist cell of Peoria, Illinois, who cares? The end result's the same. Let's just call them the buyers. They're the people at diplomatic level who make contact with the mugs on this side. They link up with the respectable people, the big shots like the man who's coming here tonight. They in turn employ a Horvis or a Braganza; at the lowest end of the scale you get the thugs who do the trigger work. The Siroccos and the Charlie Jacksons of this world. They don't even know who they're working for or why. They just line up the victims, squeeze the trigger, collect their money and leave town."

I stopped for a moment; there was a noise like a car door slamming. We strained our ears but it wasn't repeated, so I guessed it might have been the wind.

"Go on," said Dan. "I'm beginning to get interested." He leaned forward, testing the ropes that tied his hands. Sweat shone on his forehead.

"This is what I think happened," I said. "Horvis felt, as a link in the chain that he wasn't getting a big enough cut. He decided to set up his own deal. He sends out Braganza to try one of the most dangerous double crosses in the business. But

Horvis plays it smart in the Sunset Canyon caper. Hearing that his employers—the Washington or New York boys perhaps—have got wind of the deal he sends out Braganza with a briefcase filled with worthless paper.

"Sirocco and Jones, the professional hoods, have orders to liquidate the Horvis group. They trail Braganza to the Canyon and wipe him out, but the briefcase has already been passed to the Reds.

"Horvis, who has stashed the stuff away in the Chase National attempts to bluff it out with the big boys. But he gives Margaret Standish the deposit box key for safe keeping. And there's Horvis sitting on top of a pile of dynamite; in the middle with a fortune within his grasp but unable to make a move because he's watched by his own group. The documents, which deal with installations whose value will increase as time goes by, won't depreciate.

"This is the set-up when I'm called in. Horvis hopes to save his own skin by pretending to initiate his own search for the briefcase. He hopes to stave off Doomsday long enough to set up another deal. Also, by spinning me a yarn that smells from here to breakfast, he hopes that I'll be just dumb enough to play along without turning up the truth. But the top boys have sent the two hatchet men back to L.A. to put the pressure on Horvis; the group makes the wrong move, believing that I've been brought in to smoke them out. They fix Horvis, thinking that at the same time they'll frighten me off."

I stopped for a second. "They weren't doing a bad job, either," I said. Tucker allowed himself a faint smile in the intervals of straining against the ropes.

"It sounds a pretty fair construction, Mike," he said. "I'll buy it. But where does Carol Channing come in?"

"I'm working on it," I told him. "At least all the facts fit. It's the only set-up big enough to involve so many people. Why would Jacoby be mixed up in it? Would any ordinary gang risk rubbing out a police captain? And Jacoby took his orders direct from the D.A., sometimes in direct contradiction to the line you were working on."

Tucker's face looked grey. "You can't mean the D.A.——?" he began.

"I don't mean Stalin's grandmother," I told him. "This is big stuff."

"All right," he said. "This is a job for Washington and the C.I.A. boys."

"Now you're talking," I said. "This would be great if we were in L.A. Police H.Q. right now, instead of being candidates for sets of wooden underwear."

Tucker smacked his lips together like he was in pain. "Are you really sure you've got all your marbles, Mike?"

"Look," I said. "That's what everybody's been saying since the thirties. Nobody believes these things until the lid of hell blows off. Alger Hiss, Pontecorvo. . . ."

"Don't go on," he said. "I get the general idea."

He leaned his head back against the rusted mine machinery and closed his eyes. A light wind seemed to have blown up outside, lifting the humidity; it whispered over the tin roof of the hut we were lying in and it wasn't only the faint rasp over the metal that grated my nerves. I was listening intently as I leaned forward and tested the bindings that tied my hands together; I couldn't shift them. The job had been too well done and it seemed to be lengths of cable that were biting into my wrists.

There was a scuffling noise outside the hut and I knew we had only minutes, if that. I stretched again and explored the cable that bound me. It wasn't fixed to anything and I could move my hands. I knew I couldn't cut it or break it but I had an idea I might do something providing it was long enough. If I could have a few more minutes clear it might be managed. If Sirocco had tied me up and the negro hadn't noticed, we had a slim chance. I didn't know whether to make the attempt after the visitor had been or before. We might not be alive after. I told Tucker what I had in mind. He looked dubious. "I think I can work free in time if you can distract their attention," he said.

I wriggled back against the wall and felt the cable again. It was pretty tight around each wrist, but there was about three inches slack in between. It might be enough for my purposes. Trouble is, I'm a fairly tall guy and I didn't know if I could wriggle my legs through. It was a miracle they hadn't tied my ankles; then we could have sung Auf Wiedersehen for sure.

I leaned forward and then fell sideways. The blood was beginning to come back into my hands. The object of the exercise was to force my arms over my buttocks. Either my health wasn't so good or the knock on the head had been harder than I imagined. The blood pumped in my head and beads of sweat sprinkled my shirt. I felt the toe of Tucker's boot against the back of my hands. "Hold on," he said. I braced myself on the floor and tried to stay in position. He pushed hard. I felt like my hands were being torn off. Then something gave. It wasn't the wire, but I went limp and felt immediate relief. My wrists felt like they were cut and bleeding but were now in a position beneath my knees. If I couldn't get them in front of me I should be worse off than ever, because I couldn't stand or run. After resting I hunched back in a sitting position.

Tucker didn't look like he was doing much but I could sense his hands were going overtime behind his back. He was directly facing the door and couldn't make a lot of movement if there was anyone watching outside. Then I started again. I leaned back against the wall and pushed my hands down towards my ankles. I wished my legs weren't so long. At the same time I brought my right leg up and tried to hook it over my hands and the piece of wire that held them together. Without the slack I could never have done it. Sweat ran into my eyes and the room swayed. I had to stop. My heel was just caught over the wire and I stayed like this. Swell position if anyone came in.

"You know what you look like?" Tucker said calmly. He might have been home listening to the radio. "Trussed turkey isn't everyone's idea of a good meal, but——"

"Get ——," I told him, naming an impossible feat. He clicked his teeth.

"Easy to see you weren't in the Elks," he said. It relieved my feelings anyway. I made one big effort, pulled my foot up towards me; felt my knees ramming into my face. Something gave—either the cable or a tendon and I fell over backwards. A slow pain began to creep up my leg, but this was no time to slacken off; lying as I was, it was more difficult but on my back I could brace myself and rest my aching muscles. I started to move my left leg up towards the wire loop round my wrists to complete the job; the strain made impossible demands and the groan which came through my teeth surprised me.

Either I had some serious damage somewhere when I was hit over the head, or I was really out of condition. Anyway, I should find out in a few minutes. I got the heel of my left shoe over the loop and, like the other, it stuck there, with every nerve of my body shrieking; blood was running down my hands where the wire chafed it and all the weight of my left leg was making it vibrate.

I could feel my shoe slipping forwards, which was worse than useless, so I gave a desperate kick, my shoe came away quite suddenly, and I was free. I rested for a moment, smothered in dust from the floor, my wrists chafed and cut but no longer with that back-breaking strain on my arms and legs. I was lying on my back, my hands tied as before but now they were in front of me.

Like this I should have at least some sort of a chance, providing I could first find a weapon and then retain the strength to hold it. I tried to wipe my forehead on the sleeve of my jacket.

"Over there," said Tucker very slowly and calmly. Through the popping in my ears the words penetrated with difficulty. He nodded towards the door. Under the bench against which I was leaning, I could see the handle of some sort of tool. I scrabbled towards it and my hands closed over the chill of metal. I had difficulty in holding it but I pulled it back towards me and shoved it in behind me; it was a big steel bar for opening packing cases with. It would be ideal if I could use it properly;

F

it had a claw for pulling out nails and a wicked-looking spike on it. It gave me a lot of confidence.

Just then I heard somebody coming up the stairs outside. They made no attempt to conceal themselves. Whoever it was, was heavy and self-assured; I could hear the treads creak with the strain and the whole balcony seemed to vibrate. We had perhaps thirty seconds. My one chance of passing over the different position of my bound hands lay in the possibility that whoever had done it had done the job alone; if two or more men had carried it out together I was sunk.

Tucker was lying next to some old sacks. I whispered to him and he kicked them over. I picked them up and arranged the sacking in a loose bundle around me. I looped my hands under the sacking and hid them from sight. I had just eased my position and leaned back against the bench when there came a sound outside, the door opened quietly and two men came in.

4

The first was Sirocco. Behind came the big negro, Jones in Tucker's files, or whatever else he now called himself. The negro looked mean but Sirocco had on a slight smile. But it was a junky's smile, which was just as bad.

"How yo' all feelin', white trash?" the big nigger said in a sing-song voice. It was all molasses and whipped cream in its connotations but it didn't sound soft at all to me.

"You can stow that crap," I told him. "All that dialogue went out with the coon theatre way back in the days of vaudeville."

The negro came over and stood in front of me; he looked at me dispassionately. His eyes were completely expressionless. He looked pretty handy too, now that I could see him up close. He had broad shoulders like a boxer and his balled fists were like hams.

"You shouldn't have said that, white trash," he said. He moved quickly to one side and kicked me methodically in the ribs. Three times. I felt myself choking and pain stabbed up through my chest. I fell over on my side and retched. The roaring came back into my ears and the scene began to recede. It wouldn't do at all. I had to save myself for the finale. But at least it was taking the attention off Tucker.

"Had enough, gumshoe?" Sirocco asked. I didn't answer. I kept my eyes near the spot where the metal bar was hidden and bided my time.

The negro sniggered. "Suit yersel'," he said.

I caught Tucker's eye; he gave me the slightest perceptible flicker of the lids and then inclined them towards the floor. He was giving me the tip, either that his hands were free, or coming free. That was pretty good to know, anyway. If Tucker could cut loose and I could get to the iron bar when the proper time came, we might stand a chance.

"Wipe the egg off your chin," I told the nigger. "The State's hotter'n hell with all these killings. What do you think two more are going to do? The country won't be big enough to hold you."

"Yo' let us worry 'bout that, white trash," said the big punk, but he looked uneasy, all the same. Sirocco licked his lips. He might crack with a little working on, but we hadn't got the time.

"Start worrying then, Uncle Tom," I said. "The police are probably on their way up here now."

"Don't keep callin' me Uncle Tom," he flared.

"What's the matter, Uncle Tom?" I said. "Afraid?"

I thought he was going to start kicking again; he had murder in his eyes, but Sirocco caught hold of his arm.

"Mr. Gregory wants them alive, Jonesey," he said.

The big nigger shook him off "Shut up," he said. "You talk too much."

He turned back to me. "You wasn't followed up here," he said. "You was alone and you'm goin' out the same way."

"I wouldn't bet on it, Uncle Tom," I told him. "Your man at Police Headquarters is on the scram. He overreached himself."

Sirocco gulped and went white and Jones looked at me, his eyes smouldering. I followed this up quickly.

"Ask the captain," I said. They turned to Tucker. He nodded.

"Correct," he said. "Under arrest. In fact we expect to have this case under wraps within another forty-eight hours."

Sirocco mopped his face. "Look, Jonesey," he said, clutching at the negro. "I told you this whole mess would boomerang. What about lamming out; we shan't have a chance if we hang about."

The negro shook him off. "Shut up," he barked. "No need to panic. I want to think this out."

I took the opportunity to get the attention off Tucker again. His face was white and sweating and I could see that he was just about ready to slip the ropes. I rammed home my advantage quickly.

"If you get away now," I told Sirocco, "you might have a chance. But not by hanging about and certainly not by killing us."

I could see all the doubt in the world on Sirocco's face. Even the negro, tough as he was, seemed to waver, though nothing showed visibly. How it would have come out, I never knew because just at that moment, when everything hung in the balance, the noise of a motor broke the silence.

"The police——" I began, but the negro hit me a stinging slap across the mouth with his hand. I tasted blood again.

"Shut that crap," he said.

"For Chrissake," began Sirocco, but the negro silenced him with a look. With one bound he was at the light switch and plunged the shed into darkness. I heard the door creak back and as a car door slammed outside, I felt go with it the last of our hopes.

There was a shuffling on the veranda and the click of the switch; light flooded the hut again and the negro re-appeared. His face was alight with triumph.

"Mr. Gregory, right on schedule."

I looked at Dan. We exchanged bitter glances, but by the way he nodded I could tell that his wrists were free. Measured footsteps sounded on the stairs outside.

11

Gregory

THERE WAS A DEADLY SILENCE, broken only by the soft footfalls on the stairs. Sirocco went to stand by the door and the negro had his famous Luger out; it looked enormous with the silencer on. That was a gun we had to have; it was a number one priority next to our own survival. The door opened quietly and a man came into the room.

He was very tall, more than six feet and expensively, even elegantly dressed. Despite the heat he wore a long white raincoat in the Italian style; his blond hair was cropped close and very blue eyes regarded us steadily out of a long, delicate face. He had a fashionable tan and his linen and shirt cuffs were of an immaculate whiteness.

"You're sure the car is all right?" he said. He was addressing Jones, who was almost deferential as he answered the clipped, military voice.

"Perfectly, Mr. Gregory, suh," he said. "Stolen only this evening and the plates changed. No one'll ever know you was heah."

"Good," said Mr. Gregory. He turned back and gave us a hard, steady look.

"Harvard?" I asked, swapping him glance for glance. He gave a trace of a smile.

"Yale," he said. He got out a package of cigarettes; they were in some sort of expensive-looking gold and white packet.

He set fire to one with a slim gold lighter. He feathered smoke and went and sat down on a packing case. I noticed that Sirocco put a travelling rug over it before he did so.

"Now, Captain," he said, addressing Tucker. "You and your friend have given us an awful lot of trouble."

"I'm real sorry about that," said Tucker. "I'll get the L.A. Police Department to send you a letter of apology." His voice had an angry smoulder to it. Gregory laughed but there was little humour in the sound.

"You have no idea of the interests ranged against you," he said. "Compared with them, ordinary conceptions of law and order must give way."

"I've heard that somewhere before," said Tucker. "From way back. That was the old, whining yelp of crooks from Charlie Peace down to Adolf Hitler."

Gregory sighed. "This is really regrettable," he said. "My principals have the utmost regard for the capabilities of you both. I was afraid it might be a waste of time making the journey but I had to make sure."

Tucker spoke again. For some reason he had decided to take the interest off me at the moment. The three men were clustered in a semi-circle, with Tucker at the centre. From where I sat I might just make a break for the door. I felt this was what he wanted but the odds were too great. For one thing I still had some cramp in my legs. For another, it would be impossible for me to get to my feet and pick up the jemmy unnoticed; thirdly, I had the sacks wound round the lower half of my body.

The two final considerations were the most important. Jones had the big Luger with the safety catch off on a packing case within easy reach of his hand. He didn't appear to be doing anything in particular, except concentrate on the exchanges between Tucker and Gregory, but I noticed his eyes were flickering all around while they talked.

Jones could have picked up the Luger and plugged me before I got half-way to the door. And most important of all, I wasn't that much in love with death. Whatever was discussed

I was a hundred per cent certain that we were ear-marked for a single to the crematorium. This being so, it was far better to let Gregory depart before trying to make a break; that way there would only be two men to deal with.

"Fire away," Tucker told Gregory. "I'm not goin' any place."

The big negro cleared his throat. "Only one place yo' goin', white trash," he said. It sounded sinister in the semi-gloom of the hut.

"Shut your yap," Tucker told him without malice. "They're going to fry you real good and then throw away the ashes."

The negro bared his teeth in silent derision.

"It's pretty evident from our information that you and this young man know a lot about our organization," said Gregory. "We can't afford to let you live on any count but one. I hate violence and so do my principals, but too much is at stake to let normal considerations count. There is only one way in which you can continue to live——"

He broke off. Tucker was laughing quietly to himself.

"I'm wasting my time?" said Gregory.

"What do you think?" I told him.

"That you're both bloody fools," he said angrily. Two red spots stood out on his cheeks. He stood up suddenly. "We could talk this question over for hours, but I haven't the time," he said. "As it happens, there is another aspect of the case involved. I'm looking for something, Faraday, and I think you might know where it is."

"Now, let me see," I said, "My brain hasn't been so good since I fell out of my baby-carriage when I was a kid; I get all hazy sometimes."

Sirocco snittered. Gregory turned slowly to face him. I couldn't see his features but they must have been pretty expressive for the mirth turned to a yelp of pain as Jones's side-of-mutton fist closed over Sirocco's forearm.

"I cannot stand stupidity in any form," said Gregory. He turned back to me again. "Where have you put the key, Mr. Faraday?"

"What key?" I said innocently.

"The key for which my men have been searching for some considerable time," he said. "I want the information now and I want it accurately."

"You must find life very disappointing," I told him. "Bogart did this so very much better. Only even he's dead now."

Gregory shook his head impatiently. Then he smiled slowly. He had perfect teeth and it looked quite impressive. I bet he practised for hours in the mirror.

"I really would like that key," he said. His eyes weren't smiling any more. It was my turn to smile. The silence lay heavy on the air.

"You force me to take extreme measures," he said.

"You frighten me to death," I said.

"Not me," he said. "Mr. Jones."

I looked him straight in the eye. "Look, mac," I said. "I was in the Marine Corps. Prisoner of the Japs. Where they failed, do you think this goon is going to succeed?"

He turned to Tucker. "What about the captain?"

"He's a Rotarian," I said. "He couldn't possibly crack. Besides, he doesn't know where the key is, any more than you do."

Tucker snickered. Mr. Gregory sighed deeply. "You are a very difficult man to do business with, Mr. Faraday. You can't say I haven't tried."

"Sure," I said. "That will be something to console yourself with when you're back home in Washington."

It was a long shot but it went right to target. He looked at me for a long moment and his eyes were the colour of ice-water on a winter's day. Muddy ice-water too.

"You don't leave me any alternative at all, Mr. Faraday," he said slowly.

"Sure," I said. "Don't let it worry you nights."

He shrugged and looked once again from Tucker to me.

"Do you mind answering one or two questions?" I asked him. "Just for the record."

"It won't do any good," he said.

"My cussed nature," I said. "I never like to die and leave

any loose ends. I'd only lie in my coffin and worry about it for a coupla centuries."

Sirocco would have sniggered again but I could see Uncle Tom was standing too close to him.

"This espionage ring. . . ." I began. Gregory stopped me with an abrupt motion of his hand. His tan had gone white around the nostrils and his breath was coming fast. He put his hand into his inside coat pocket.

"Don't give too much away, Mr. Faraday," he said. "We mustn't let the hired help into the State secrets. Otherwise, the unpleasantness will have to be right now."

I bit back my words. We stared at one another for a couple of long seconds. Finally he pulled out his hand from his outside pocket and selected another cigarette from his pack.

"All right," I said. "Make it in ciphers if you like. Your crowd had Horvis on the payroll but he crossed you. You couldn't find the goods, suspected that Horvis had stashed them but couldn't prove it. Stalemate. So, to put you off the scent, he hired me on a pretence of doing some investigations in a false direction. Correct?"

"More or less," he said.

"Good," I told him. "What made our friends kill him? We know they were responsible for Braganza, Jacoby and one or two others."

Mr. Gregory looked from me to Tucker and back again with something like admiration. "It's a great shame you won't join us. A shocking waste of talent. Why did we kill him? Quite simple, really. Information had come into our hands that resolved all doubt—we have many sources, a great deal of information passes to us through official channels.

"We knew Horvis had a key; we suspected to a bank deposit box or vault, but we couldn't find out which bank, city or branch. We got tired of Horvis; he was altogether too clever and we had played along with him too long. The organization was in jeopardy; why take risks? We liquidated him and implicated you; we could quite easily find the key ourselves, or that was the general idea. Until recently."

"Was that when I began to get too troublesome?" I said.

"You may rightly flatter yourself, Mr. Faraday," he said. "You were quite troublesome, right from the beginning. I have the greatest respect for your methods; methods obviously tempered in a hard school. These men were getting somewhat careless and stupid. Though you had a certain amount of luck—you are the first man Jones shot at with intent who escaped, and his second effort at your own office, again met with ill success, illustrates how extraordinarily chance may intervene in even the most smoothly organized operations."

"And Jacoby and Paul Mellow?" I said. "Jacoby, the desk sergeant Clark, probably the D.A. himself—all tied in."

He smiled again. "That shouldn't have been too difficult for you, Mr. Faraday. Jacoby had his uses but he began to panic when the heat was on. We had to shut him up and our treatment of Mellow was pretty effective, as you have seen. He hasn't said a word yet, has he, captain?"

Dan was still lying with his head down and his eyes closed, as though exhausted. He shook himself like an old, lame dog and looked about him with an effort. Even I was almost taken in. It was pretty good play-acting.

"He will," said Dan, without opening his eyes. "Come his trial he'll sing as pretty as any nightingale. And then your whole organization will start cracking up. They always do; the trail will lead to you and then your superiors. The trials will last about a year, I'd say and the jails'll be full to burstin'.

"Unless you plan to rub out the hatchet men first; you'd have to do that, I guess, and the link men, otherwise everything would trace back. And that wouldn't do, would it?"

There was an ugly silence and I saw Sirocco and Uncle Tom exchange looks. I thought Gregory's laugh was somewhat nervous. Anyway, his reaction was rather too slow.

"I'd like to go along with you on that, Captain," he said, "but practice hasn't borne out your theory. The democratic citizen himself inhibits that. He's paralysed by collective fear. And when the democratic system breaks down, as it's doing all over the West, then the bold, the strong, the opportunists step in."

I expected Dan to generate some heat at this, but to my surprise he kept his eyes closed. "People like you make me puke," he told Gregory. "See you in the chair."

Gregory's face twitched slightly. "We're wasting time, gentlemen," he said crisply.

"Thanks for looking in," I said. His face set like stone. He looked at his wrist watch.

"No longer than ten minutes," he said to Uncle Tom. "Then get the hell out."

The negro nodded. "Don't you worry, boss," he rumbled. "We ain't aimin' to make a career round heah."

Gregory moved over to the door. He hesitated a moment, with his fingers on the handle.

"See you in the morgue," said Tucker. Gregory's face remained blank.

"I want to speak to you," he told Uncle Tom. "Keep your eyes peeled," he said sharply to Sirocco. The latter nodded and leaned against the wall. The two men went out. We could hear their foosteps going down the stairs. It was now or never.

2

Sirocco hadn't got his gun out. He had no need of it. We were ostensibly two half insensible, beat-up men, trussed like chicken and just waiting for the kill. He looked at me and smiled. I felt it was time to get moving. I looked at Dan. He half grinned. Then he nodded. There was just one more thing we were waiting for. It came two seconds afterwards. A door slammed, a car engine started and Gregory's car gunned out of the yard.

From then on in things started to happen in a hurry. Tucker's hands came out from behind his back and he went in a long, crawling rush towards Sirocco. I caught a glimpse of him; he had his mouth and his eyes wide open. Then he went down in a splintering of wood as the whole weight of

Tucker's massive body caught him behind the knees. I saw Sirocco's gun hand was half in his coat pocket before Dan's hand closed over his arm.

Then I had to work hard myself. I threw away the sacks, found I could stand without feeling dizzy. I got the iron bar firmly clasped in my two hands and shuffled over towards the door. Tucker and Sirocco were rolling over and over and there was a hell of a lot of noise going on. I could hear the thunder of the negro's feet on the stairs and I knew he'd have his gun out when he came through the door.

I braced myself against the wall, steadied the jemmy in my hands, which the wire rope strengthened, and put one foot out in front of me. I didn't want to be brained by the back-lash of the door when Uncle Tom burst through it. I didn't have long to wait. Dan Tucker and Sirocco were swapping violence on the floor when Uncle Tom took the door in his stride; he looked about a mile high and just as broad when he ripped it back on its hinges. The lock went one way and I felt a stabbing pain in my toe; I thought it might be broken but I didn't have time to worry about that.

Jones had the Luger out as he came through; I brought my clenched hands over and hit his hand with all the strength I could muster. I saw blood burst through the broken skin, the big negro grunted and the gun went skittering along the floor. That was my first worry over; my second, and biggest was the strength of this coon. Any normal person's arm would have been broken and he'd only grunted. I followed him up from behind, flailing at his head with my iron bar; I'd got it pretty securely held and I felt a couple of good ones thud on his skull.

They just bounced off. Guess his dome must have been made of pure rock. Uncle Tom grunted again, this time with sur-prise as well as pain; I kicked him in the back as we went waltzing down the room and I got in another hard one across the thick of his neck as he went crashing full tilt into a steel pulley block that protruded from the quarry machinery. The last blow had hit home; I felt the bar sink in. I had put every ounce of strength into it with the hope of breaking his neck.

But this wasn't a normal man. It was far from mortal but that one he felt. Out of the corner of my eye I could see Tucker and the junky rolling over against the rusted mine machinery and I heard Sirocco groan once; but I was too busy to take much more notice. When he felt the weight of my iron bar, Uncle Tom seemed to go mad. He writhed like an epileptic and then went up towards the ceiling like a rocket; I stepped back in case he was fooling and caught him one across the kidneys as he went by.

There was foam on his lips and his eyes were full of raving madness but his face was curiously calm. As he crashed back across the room I could hear a strange noise from between his clenched teeth. For the first time I began to feel afraid. Uncle Tom was singing to himself as he fought; warming to his work. I had noticed this peculiarity among some negroes before but it was the first time I had experienced it in person. It wasn't pleasant.

Uncle Tom came at me then with his fists flailing; I caught him on the knuckles again with the iron bar, but one of his balled hands caught me a glancing blow on the side of the head. It was probably a love pat for him but it was a five megaton punch for me. Flashes of light mingled with the brilliant technicolor fireworks. Then I went back against an iron girder jutting out from the wall and skyrockets added to the beauty of the night.

More seriously, as I put out my hands to save myself they ripped against the rusted metal; the iron bar came unhooked from my hands and went clanging down the length of the room. I hit dirt and a numb despair came into my mind. The negro went after the iron bar like a cat. I heard Dan Tucker or Sirocco make a choking noise. The nigger crouched on his heels and felt for the bar.

"Your death come now, white trash," he whistled through his teeth. I put my shoulder against the wall and levered myself roofwards. The negro stood up. He still looked about a mile tall and twice as wide even from the other end of the room. I balanced my hands on the floor and prepared to shove. It was then that Dan Tucker got to the Luger. There was a grating noise along the floor as he slid it to me. The wire round my wrists chinked and I felt the reassuring coldness of it against my hands.

I held it between my two hands and got upright just as Uncle Tom started his run in towards me. I knew the safety catch wouldn't be on so it was no risk. Even so, I thought I'd give him the chance he'd never given anyone else.

"Drop it, Uncle Tom, less you want two ass-holes," I told him.

"Gonna kill you, white trash," he said for the last time. I nodded and put a slug in his right shoulder. The gun sighed as I squeezed the trigger. A large hole stencilled itself in the nigger's shirt front; the big slug flung him against the wall but he kept on coming.

I gave him another in the gut and as he lifted one leg in front of another, one in the belly; he was almost on me now and still lifting the iron bar so I gave him a fourth in the heart. He made a loud groan and scarlet froth bubbled out of his lips. There was a crash like the fall of doom as he hit the floor. Then I gave him another one, for Bert Dexter, as he lay there.

"Jeezechrise," said Tucker in the heavy silence. "Some coon."

I could see Sirocco's eyes white as marble straining from a face like a death's head, pinioned under Tucker's massive arm. I thought he was just frightened until I found his neck was broken. Like me, Dan had to make sure.

The thin wail of sirens began to fill the night air, coming up the valley towards the quarry. I let the Luger fall to the ground with a thump and the silencer broke off as it hit the floor.

"I could do with a cigarette," I said to no one in particular.

I went to the door and waited for the prowl cars to arrive.

3

We drank coffee someone had thoughtfully produced from flasks. The big room was full of cops, the yard overflowed with gunning motors and spotlights stabbed across the windows and around the sheds down below. Stella's face looked white and anxious as she sat opposite me with McGiver. Dan Tucker, starting his third apple with relish, winced as he paused in rattling out instructions, and fingered his wrists. For the second time—things didn't seem to be getting through to my consciousness very well—I repeated our story to Stella.

I put my teeth on the rim of my coffee cup and savoured the hot liquid. It smarted against my cut mouth but that didn't matter now.

"How did you find out?" I asked Stella. She shot a glance at McGiver.

"Sergeant Clark got a bit too clever," said McGiver. "He'd been told to get you and the captain out here. But he thought it would be better if your secretary were included. He rang Stella—in confidence of course. Said you wanted to see her. She didn't leave it at that. She rang back to check on something about a half hour later, on her way across town. Unfortunately for Clark he had gone off duty, so the call was put through to me by the relief desk sergeant. Then we added things up and got the hell out here."

"And Clark?" I asked.

"He's been arrested already," he said. "He gave us a couple of other names. Looks like we're having a new D.A. too."

"What was Clark's idea in exceeding his instructions?" I asked McGiver.

He smiled. "He was on the look-out for promotion," he said. "In the organization, of course, not the force. He thought his employers would be pleased with him for turning Stella over."

"Like hell they will," I said.

"Have you got road blocks out for Gregory?" I asked Tucker. "And you'd better ring the airport."

"Relax," said Tucker. "That was on the air within five seconds of their arrival. The whole State's sewn up by now. It may take all night, though, if Gregory's managed to change cars; he might even bluff his way through a cordon if he's high up enough in Washington."

I looked across at the two shapes under the sheets in the other corner of the room. Flash bulbs were still going and a ballistics sergeant went by with Jones's Luger wrapped in a piece of cloth.

"Tell the labs I want a complete report in an hour," Tucker told him.

"Right," said Peters and went out briskly.

"I haven't had a chance to say anything, Mike, but thanks," said Dan as he passed me. He rested his hand on my shoulder for a moment.

"We'll talk about it in our rocking chairs at the police smoker," I told him. I grinned at Stella. She still looked anxious but the paleness had gone from her face. I got up clumsily, found I was aching all over and hobbled to one side with Tucker.

"How will this affect Paul Mellow's end?" I asked him. "I'd like to let Mandy know how things are making out—just to round off the case."

Tucker's face creased into a brief smile. He crunched another apple. "You can tell Mandy I think he'll draw a suspended sentence. And tell him to keep the boy out of trouble in future."

As I turned back to Stella, the door opened and Mac-Namara came in. He took one look round the room, sniffed, and came on over. He surveyed the two sheeted bodies and glanced at me.

"Do you have to kill people during the night?" he asked sourly.

"This is the third evening I've been called out in a row."

"Sorry," I said. "I'll remember that in future. We'll give you time and a half."

To my surprise he smiled thinly. I thought the front of his

face was going to fall off. "Come and sit over here," he said. "I'd better have a look at you."

He went over me. He whistled when he saw my hands. I winced when he pressed against my ribs.

"I think you got a couple of cracked ones," he said. "I'll tape you up to make sure."

Inside fifteen minutes I began to look like something out of a B horror film. With bandages round my wrists too, I was quite a sight.

"You'd better get your own doctor to run over you in a day or two," he said. "Otherwise you're as good as new."

I thanked him. Then he went over and pulled the sheets back from the two bodies on the floor. He was silent for a moment. He prodded the negro with his toe.

"Looks like he died of bullet wounds," he said.

"Tell me something new," said Dan. "Want a complete autopsy report on both by morning. Watch for wrist powder burns from that Luger on the nigger, that's important."

MacNamara looked at his wrist watch and sighed. "Why the delay?" he said. "I thought you were going to ask me for the paper work in half an hour."

"We don't believe in overworking the staff," said Dan. He clapped him on the shoulder as he went by. MacNamara winced. As we went out the door he was already putting on a white apron. I stumbled and Stella put her hand on my arm. McGiver stayed to direct operations. The yard was full of cops and cars. The night air smelt good as we went down the stairs.

"This is better than being carried down," said Dan with enthusiasm.

"They'd never have carried you down," I said. Dan's laugh boomed in the night. There was still quite a heat in the atmosphere, not quite dispersed in the light wind from the hills. Spotlight beams from the cars were stabbing paths in the bushes and curious faces were turned up at us out of the darkness. Two big white ambulances pulled in at the entrance to the quarry as we got down to the ground.

"All right, Bish," said Tucker as a brawny-looking patrolman saluted him. "Take Mr. Faraday's car and follow us back to town. You're not fit to drive," he added to me. I nodded. Truth to tell I felt pretty bushed and the rest on the way back would set me up for the night.

"Perhaps you'd get in back, miss," said Tucker, opening the rear door for Stella. I got in the right hand front seat next to Tucker and sat staring at the fly smears on the windscreen. It felt like a million years since I'd enjoyed the luxury of leather seats and contemplation. I wondered how Mr. Gregory would feel when he realized that his plan had misfired; more important, who Mr. Gregory was. For all we knew he might be in custody already, although we should have heard on Tucker's car radio.

A big chunky cop I hadn't seen before got in back with Stella and slammed his door. He smiled at me sympathetically. I heard the scratch of a match in back and the flare of it made a momentary glow in the darkness round the car. I caught a brief glimpse of myself in the glass of the windscreen. I looked real beat up. I sneaked a look at my watch. To my surprise it was only a quarter to one; barely three hours since I had first hit the dirt road to the quarry. I felt at least ten years older.

The lights of L.A. were shimmering through the blur some miles off. My ribs twinged. Tucker went around to the driving seat and got in. He was breathing heavily and I felt the glove locker click as he reached in for an apple. I couldn't help grinning to myself in the gloom. I fingered my ribs again and came up against my empty holster.

"That reminds me," I said to Dan. "Did you see what happened to my Smith-Wesson after I dropped?"

He grunted. He handed me something metallic across the seat. Butt first.

"Safety catch on," he said. "We took it off Jones afterwards."

"Thanks," I said. "I don't feel properly dressed without this."

I put it back in the holster. I expected it might feel heavy against my ribs but the bulk of it there in the webbing seemed to smooth the pain away.

"Where to?" I said.

"Headquarters first," he answered. "When it gets light we'll take the Chase National. And we ought to contact Washington as soon as possible."

Dan gunned the motor and we turned out of the quarry entrance, tyres scuffing on the gravel. A cop standing by a patrol car at the entrance saluted. In the mirror I could see the lights of my own car behind. There were two cops in it. As we came out on to the dirt road I could see more lights in the top of the quarry building and men in white coats climbing the staircase. The night air felt suddenly cool on my cheek as we went down the road. Dan didn't use the siren and there was a remarkable peace. It didn't last for long.

We had gone about two miles down the twisting track from the summit. Dan had pulled way ahead of my own car for he wanted to get back to town as quickly as possible. The Buick hadn't got the pace anyway, and I was glad the patrolman driving hadn't tried to pull up level as the dirt road wouldn't have improved the springs any, and I didn't want the engine flogged. We had just passed a point where the dirt road branched into another which led way off into the hills. I was looking idly out of the window on my side, puffing my cigarette, when I saw two dark shapes some way back from the road. They looked like cars.

As we passed, side-lights winked on one of the dark shapes and a few seconds later the car had pulled on to the road behind us. I didn't fall in for a moment or two. Dan Tucker hadn't noticed anything; he had his eyes on the verge ahead. We had come to a part where there was a pretty big gully down into the brush and underscrub at the roadside and there were one or two nasty rock formations jutting out. It occurred to me that Dan might have thought the car behind was mine, when suddenly it began to accelerate.

I just had time to tell Dan, "We got company," when a

blinding glare etched everything in the car with the light of day. I glanced back and saw that the car behind, a cream roadster had a big spotlight on the screen upright switched on.

"What the hell——" Dan began when there was a bang from behind; I thought we'd burst a tyre and then the back window of the prowl car disintegrated into a thousand starred facets and something buried itself in the upholstery with an ugly thud.

"Get down," I yelled to Stella and everyone flattened themselves to the floor, except Tucker, who had to go on grimly steering. He told me afterwards he felt as big as a barn door up there in the glare of the light.

"Get over into the middle of the road," I told Dan. As he pulled the big car over I could get the cream job clearly in view. I couldn't be absolutely sure but there was only one figure in the car and the white raincoat clinched it.

"It's Gregory," I shouted to Tucker.

"Persistent cuss, ain't he?" he ground out. "See if you can do something about that spot before he alters the shape of my spine."

I got the Smith-Wesson out and lined up on a point about a foot above the driver's head and to the left of the pursuing car. He got off another shot at that second, but it must have gone wide, because Dan had started weaving across the road. I hoped there weren't any couples sitting in cars parked without lights up ahead. As soon as Dan stopped his criss-cross and steadied I loosed off a shot. The gun coughed and Gregory's car swerved convulsively but the light didn't go out; then I saw that the windscreen had gone, but the figure in white was sitting bolt upright in the moonlight, apparently unharmed.

"Weave again and then steady up," I told Dan. "Shout when you're ready."

The cop in the rear offside seat with Stella had got his revolver out, but he hadn't had any chance to use it because he was sitting too far over.

"There's a tommy-gun under the seat," said Tucker to the

patrolman, as though reading my thoughts. "Use it if you have to, but for Chrissake get that light out."

I took one look at the speedometer before I turned back to face the rear. We were already doing more than sixty and if we hit a rock at that speed on this rutted, poorly made road, verged by dangerous ravines, anything could happen. Dan swerved as Gregory fired again; I caught the stab of fire, but the bullet apparently got the bodywork of our car and was deflected. As Dan straightened up I got in a burst of three, quick shots, shifting them upwards and outwards to stitch across the windscreen. There was a vivid cracking noise which I could hear even above our engine and then the spot suddenly went out with a loud bang and a puff of smoke.

The sports job swerved and then, just as quickly, the headlamps came on brilliantly and flicked up to full beam. Gregory was pretty good, I had to give him that. When I turned again I could hardly believe my eyes. Gregory was accelerating straight for the back of the prowl car.

"Watch it, Dan," I said. "Looks like he's going to ram us."

As I spoke Tucker put his foot on the accelerator. We slammed back in the seats as the big car thrust forward, but it wasn't quite enough. With an angry howl the cream sports job cannoned into the back of us. There was a heavy crunch, a squeal of tyres and the prowl car lurched sideways crazily with the impact; I caught a glimpse of the sports job dropping back, one wing crumpled and then the offside front headlight went out.

Dan Tucker had done a fine job in straightening the careening car but there was an ominous lop-sidedness about the steering and the stench of burning rubber was only too evident. I guessed some part of the bodywork was scraping one of the back wheels and a blow-out would be only a matter of time.

"He's really out to get us, ain't he?" said Tucker to nobody in particular.

Stella flashed me a quick, frightened smile. I saw she had got her fingers crossed. Dan straightened the car and then started to weave as the sports job pulled up again. I could still see Gregory grim and hunched as he came in to the attack, and I had a momentary flash of grudging admiration. It was a Spartan attitude in a way; sacrifice for the good of the system.

"Hold on," said Tucker, crouching low over the wheel. "I'm going to try something. There's a lay-by about a quarter of a mile farther down. It's on the off-side of the road and I'm going to take him by surprise. I'm trying to get in at speed, stop quickly and let him overrun."

He turned back quickly to the big patrolman. "Got that tommy, Stevens?" he said between his teeth. "You'd better change places with the young lady. Give it to him when he goes by. We've got to stop him for good. We shan't get two chances."

There was a metallic click as the big cop started breaking out the tommy-gun; the L.A. boys usually have one or two surprises like this, stashed in cases on the floor of their cars. I heard a clip go home with a sweetly-oiled snick, and then the seat springs gave as the two changed over. There was a squeak as Stevens wound the window down. I had nothing to do now because I couldn't shoot; Stevens's head was in the way and the car's rear window was now too bullet-starred to see through.

Gregory didn't fire again though, and as Dan had his toe down he wasn't able to get quite as close. The dust of the road swirled in at the windows as we screamed down the hill road at what I should normally have regarded as suicidal speed and the lights of L.A. seemed to be coming up fast. It was a sticky fifteen seconds before Tucker pulled way over to the right, to his own side of the road.

"Hold on, everybody," he said suddenly. "We're going in. Stand by Stevens, and let him have it when you're ready."

I just had time to jam myself down in my seat and brace my hand against the door handle, before the car made a sickening swerve; it was so sharp that I thought we were going over. I heard a startled exclamation from Stella, who was lying prone on the floor at the rear; metal banged on glass just behind my head and my own gun fell with a muffled thud on to the carpet.

I caught a glimpse of lights and bushes whirling and marvelled at the calmness of Dan Tucker spinning the wheel. There was a horrifying bang that rose the hair on my scalp as we spun off the road, made a U-turn and went screaming along the lay-by. Through the window I could see an ugly ravine coming up too fast.

Then tyres tore on dirt and rock and Dan was putting on the brakes. The manœuvre had fooled Gregory all right. I risked a glimpse through the window and saw the big sports job tearing by level with us. Gregory was pulling at the wheel but it was obvious he would have to stay on the road, for he hadn't a hope of getting in and remaining alive.

"Right!" yelled Dan as we went into a long skid. Stones and small boulders banged and rattled along the car body as we ploughed across the lay-by and into the scree. There was a deafening bang as Stevens opened up with the tommy-gun. Streaks of light went lancing towards the cream sports job and a shower of sparks shot into the night sky.

Cartridge cases were raining down over the seat on to the back of my neck and the stench of cordite fumes and smoke was beginning to fill the car. As we went lurching and sprawling towards the gully, Dan straightened up and started applying the brake again and Stevens got in a short, second burst. I caught a fractional glimpse of Gregory's white-coated figure before it slumped like a marionette with cut strings and the big sports left the road in a sheet of flame.

The steering, jammed by the weight of the body, carried the car in a wide arc like a meteorite and blazing petrol made a comet-tail on the grass behind it. It went into a thicket of small trees with a truly impressive roar and then turned over. The blazing ruins of the automobile went skittering on and then fell in what might perhaps have been a forty feet trajectory into the ravine below.

A dozen trees went up like match sticks in the resultant explosion and flame rained skywards. Small boulders kept clattering towards the ravine bed as choking black smoke blossomed out above the tree tops. Dan brought the car to a shuddering stop and it was suddenly quiet. The crackling of flames and fierce heat catching the tree branches were an intrusion into the silence. We sat looking down on the cremation.

"Nice driving," said Stevens, breaking a difficult pause. Dan nodded as he reached into the glove compartment for his bag of apples.

"Nice shooting," he told Stevens. The tones of the two men were gravely professional.

Stella's white face appeared from behind the back of the seat and her hand sought mine. We sat there looking down at the pyre. Like I said, it was a Spartan finish.

12

Mr. Stich

It was around a quarter to two the next afternoon when Tucker tooled a patrol job into the parking lot of the Bissell Building. As far as I knew Carol Channing was an innocent, but there were a few loose ends and the Ralph Johnson angle, coupled with her lies still stuck out like a plate of oatmeal biscuits in a slaughter house.

"Half an hour," said Tucker. He leaned back in the seat of the prowl car and put on a pair of sun glasses. With his sunburn he looked like a short-sighted side of beef.

"Right," I said, slamming the car door. An apple-core hit the dust before I had gone a dozen yards and I could hear his teeth get to work on a second. Admiral Dewey almost bent double opening the main doors for me. I figured he'd be in line for the Congressional Medal if he kept this up. I rode up in the lift and then drifted along the corridor.

There were a lot of corpses between now and last time, but we had most of the answers straight. I hit the door buzzer. There was silence except for the humming of the air-conditioning. Sweat trickled down my shirt-band. It always did since this case began. The silence was unbroken and I was about to hit the buzzer again when the door was opened.

Carol looked stunning. In fact, I couldn't remember a time when she didn't. She wore a cream suit with an open-necked shirt and she had a pale pink scarf at her throat. She had on crocodile skin shoes to match the suit and carried a handbag to match the shoes. Some doll. As she opened the door I took in the pile of crocodile skin luggage on the carpet beyond. That matched too.

"Going somewhere, darling?" I said.

She flushed. Her smile was as sincere as a politician's on election night.

"Just getting ready to leave in the morning," she said, forcing the words out of her mouth. "I didn't expect you until much later."

"Obviously," I said, pushing my way through the door and closing it behind me. She gave back a couple of feet then and I was able to see the room more clearly. There were a couple of trunks, a holdall and a white raincoat. She was certainly on the move all right.

"You've seen the papers?" I said.

"Yes," she said brightly. "You did a good job, Mike."

She sauntered rather too casually over to the centre of the room and lit a cigarette. I didn't offer to light it for her. The magic had gone; besides, I don't go for that sort of stuff in the afternoons.

"You wanted to see me specially?" she asked.

"I thought you'd want a breakdown on the case," I said. She went and sat on the divan and crossed her legs carefully. She looked worried, as though she couldn't place something. I thought she looked like she was listening for somebody.

"Expecting company?" I asked.

"Of course not," she said sharply. "You know I don't know anybody except you in L.A."

I shrugged. I crossed over to the divan and sat down in an easy chair opposite her. I studied her face, but she wasn't giving anything away. I took out my pocket book. I showed her the initials written in it.

"These mean anything to you?" I asked. She studied it nonchalantly, but I felt, rather than saw her face going white under its natural colour.

"Seems like CRTIS," she said, with what looked like an assumed calmness. "What's your theory?"

"So far as I have one," I said. "I figure that perhaps Horvis —or maybe Braganza, though it's not likely in his case— decided to leave a clue to the identity of the Big Wheel on certain incriminating documents. Then, when the police found them, they would know who to go for."

She wrinkled her nose. "It figures. But why are you telling me all this, Mike?"

"Because you might be able to help," I said.

She looked surprised. "Meaning you don't think I'm on the level?"

I looked round the apartment. "Meaning I don't think you intended to stay over Christmas," I said. She smiled faintly.

"I got all the information I wanted out of the papers," she said. "We can leave all the rest to the L.A. police. I got what I came for. Ralph's murderers have paid up. That's all I'm interested in. Frankly, I didn't want to see you again after everything was over. We got too . . . involved. And I've got other plans."

"So I see," I said.

She ruffled up. "You don't believe me?" she said. I shrugged again. She pointed to the table.

"I hadn't forgotten you, if that's what you're worried about. There's a cheque there, addressed in a stamped envelope to you, ready for mailing."

"I didn't mean that," I said, pulling my big bluff. "We've got the kingpin," I said. "He's singing like a nightingale. And he's implicated you from here to Honolulu. Tucker wants you brought in for questioning. Then we're all going to take a trip to Washington."

For a minute I thought she was going to hit me. She went white and took one step forward with her arm raised in the air. Her face worked for a couple of seconds and her eyes looked like a cornered ferret. She almost spat when she spoke.

"All right," she said eventually, almost in a whisper. "If that's the way it's got to be. Ortis isn't the only one who'll be doing any singing. I've got enough information about the whole ring to send a couple of hundred people to Leavenworth for about fifty thousand years."

Jackpot first time. I was finding the truth interesting—even though it was a little late. Seemed I had the name of a big fish, though Ortis conveyed nothing to me. Carol Channing seemed to have forgotten my presence. She dabbed furiously at her face with a square of linen and then fumbled in her handbag.

"Give me a light, Mike, will you?" she said. I obliged and she sucked furiously at the end of the cigarette.

"What do you think they'll do to me?" she said at last.

I hadn't a hell of an idea what she was talking about or how she tied in with the story, but I kept her stringing along.

"We might make a deal," I said soberly, "providing you sing loud enough."

She nodded and drew on the cigarette again. "I suppose there's no chance of me being able to duck out?" she asked. "You've got what you want. One more or less won't make a lot of difference. Won't you give me a break, Mike?"

She looked into my eyes. "Maybe," I said convincingly. We were standing quite close together. Her mouth met mine and her tongue was boring into my mouth like a snake. I had one breast cupped and the other hand behind her. So it was easy just to clamp my fingers over her wrist as she put her hand into the handbag. She gave a muffled yell and a small nickel-plated revolver bounced down to the carpet between our feet. I held her close with my other arm and finished off the kiss. Then I pushed her away.

Her eyes were blazing. "You lousy ——" she said. Even I couldn't repeat what she said. "Of all the lowdown tricks." She spat in my face before I could move. I felt the saliva dribble down my cheek. I looked steadily into her eyes as I reached for my handkerchief. I kept my foot on the gun, for she would have used it, the mood she was in.

"Too bad it had to end this way, darling," I said. "I feel you've broken a mood of golden enchantment."

I should have left it at that, but as usual I overdid things. The look on her face should have warned me but the faint shadow at the corner of my eye clinched it. I ducked rapidly, for a slugging twice in twenty-four hours is too much even for me to take. It was graceful stuff but it didn't win the competition.

Something heavy missed my head, but struck my shoulder a savage blow, sending me to the carpet, every nerve shrieking. Through the fireworks I could see the Channing girl and the feet of a big man in tan brogues; the couple gathered up the cases in five seconds flat and a moment later I heard the balcony door shut softly behind them. Then, through the cotton wool I heard a car sneak stealthily away. I lay fighting nausea and slowly drifted out to sea.

Dan Tucker found me there five minutes later, when he poked his head round the door. I was feeling better then, but I didn't get up. I took one look at his disgusted face and closed my eyes again. Whatever I said wouldn't have done any good and the explanations could wait till later.

2

I sat in my office, put my feet up on the desk and looked up at the ceiling. It was still as hot as hell. There was a big, new cream-painted partition across one side of my office, which was now half the size. I still couldn't get used to it. My door had been replaced. It was a solid oak job with no glass panel. The lock had been changed too.

I didn't know the new man at the insurance company. We just said good morning or good night whenever we met in the corridor. It was probably best that way. I looked across the desk to where Stella stood near the partitioned-off area. She was brewing more coffee, though why I wouldn't know. It only made me hotter still. I sweated as the thought and looked over at the corner window. The spider was gone from his usual position. Even he was off the case. I sighed again and glanced down at the big earthenware ash-tray on the far side of my desk. Tucker's two apple cores were rapidly turning brown.

The late edition was spread out on the desk top. PENTAGON CHIEF RICHTER DIES it said in letters two feet deep. ADMIRAL'S HEART ATTACK IN OFFICE it said underneath. But the Big Wheel had undoubtedly bitten on his poison phial when the going got too hot.

"And who was this Colonel Ortis?" Stella asked.

"The Admiral's sidekick," I said. "As it turned out, the old coot in the pink slacks I saw playing tennis shots next to the Horvis house. They rented the place adjoining to keep an eye on him. Some nerve. Gregory was their front man."

Stella frowned. "And Carol Channing?" she went on.

"She was Ortis's mistress originally but she was two-timing him with the Johnson lad," I said, smoking as I scanned the paper. "They got Johnson into the espionage racket as his technical ability was useful to them, but at some stage he threatened to turn Ortis in to the police. The old boy put the dogs on him. The Channing girl couldn't prove Ortis had anything to do with his death but she started her own investigations for revenge. Her feelings were genuine enough so far as that went."

Stella was silent as she drank her coffee and then she returned to the attack.

"But I still don't get the last angle? Who slugged you and how was he connected with Channing?"

"Ah, there I can help you," I said. "Tucker just filled in that piece. Party name of Saul Chaplin. Yet another of Carol's boy-friends. To be precise he was Ortis's personal secretary at the Pentagon and in charge of the payroll. Somehow Carol got wind that the whole caboodle was caving in and he came out to L.A. to pick her up."

I didn't tell her that Chaplin and Carol had disappeared with a quarter of a million dollars worth of Government paper money. That wasn't in the papers either. Carol had given Chaplin the alarm just before the organization's pay night. Convenient for them. My guess was that they wouldn't be found with that sort of money to buy them immunization.

Not that I had done badly myself. The cheques kept rolling

in. There was one from Mandy Mellow with a note; I'd already cashed Carol Channing's. There was another invitation too from Margaret Standish but I hadn't taken it up. The biggest surprise was the cheque from Uncle Sam; I'd better not say how much it was for, or the Chamber of Commerce would start squawking about the waste of their taxes. But it was enough to start me thinking about buying a new car and taking a holiday in Florida. I felt I needed it.

"I'm still not quite sure why those two boys roughed up the Channing girl," said Stella.

"Ortis was trying to warn her off," I said, my mind on other things. Stella nodded. I smoked on. The only detail that fidgeted me was what had really happened to Carol and the he-man; and how they had swung the deal. I can't say I was sorry at the way things had turned out. Ortis had it coming and she really was a good-looker. Stella came back and put some more coffee in front of me.

"There you are, boss," she said with deceptive humility. She sat down in her chair opposite and looked at me quizzically. "Just what was there between you and the Channing girl, Mike?" she said. "Or shouldn't I ask?"

"You'll find it all in my notes," I said with bland evasiveness.

"You wouldn't put that sort of stuff in," she said. "I looked."

I got up to pinch her bottom but she was too quick for me.

"Look. . . ." I said, absently trying to peck her on the side of the cheek and drink my cup of coffee simultaneously.

"You'd better put that down," she said. "You can only do one thing properly at a time."

"What I was thinking. . . ." I said a while afterwards, straightening my tie. . . ." we both need a holiday. I'm not due in Washington until late fall. Three weeks in Florida wouldn't do either of us any harm."

"That sounds nice, Mike," she said, kissing me again. This one was more formal but it still set me tingling all the way down to my socks.

"Expenses paid?" she said.

"Expenses paid," I said.

She went and sat down at the desk again and l
walls.

"Just thinking what to wear," she said. "It'l
Florida."

"That'll be a change," I said.

Just then the phone rang. Stella picked it up.
it to me.

"My name is Elihu Q. Stich," said a prissy vo
and handed the phone back to Stella. She put he
the mouthpiece and turned back to me.

"His mother-in-law's missing. He wants you

"He must be nuts," I said.

Stella took down a few notes and then hung
smoked and puzzled out that loose end. As it
didn't get the answer until some while after, wher
from Florida, which is another story.

It came in the mail. There seemed to be more
bills these days, which made a change. I sat adm
in the telephone mirror and sifting the letters. I
at the bottom.

It was just a card with a coloured view, and
words on the reverse. It said, "Have fun, Mike
million dollars. Wish you were here."

She didn't sign it, but she didn't have to. The
Nicaragua. I passed the card to Stella to read. I
listening to the traffic on the boulevard. It was sti
to get hotter.

Funny thing about Carol. You never can tell
The card put the last piece on the board.

I didn't tell Tucker. It wouldn't have done a
I had to think of his ulcers. It wasn't really Nic
know it was some place where they wouldn't thir
in a million years.